Jeff Petert.1
7-67

W9-AXG-063

JAMES PURDY was born in Ohio in 1927
and was educated at the University of
Chicago, the University of Puebla in Mexico,
and the University of Madrid. In 1958 he
won a Guggenheim Fellowship for creative
writing and a National Institute of Arts and
Letters award. He now lives in Brooklyn
Heights. The consistently high quality of his
work and his rapidly growing international
reputation led *The New York Times* to call
him "one of the most decisive literary tal-
ents to have appeared since the last war."

His first work, COLOR OF DARKNESS, a
collection of short stories, appeared in 1957,
and a second collection, CHILDREN IS ALL,
in 1962. Both appear in a single Avon edition. In addition to THE NEPHEW, his other
novels, MALCOLM, published in 1959, and
CABOT WRIGHT BEGINS, 1964, are also
available in Avon editions.

AVON BOOK DIVISION
The Hearst Corporation
572 Madison Avenue
New York 22, N. Y.

THE Nephew

JAMES PURDY

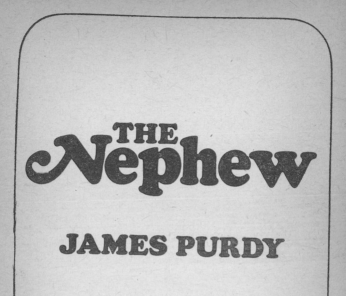

An Avon Library Book

For: John Cowper Powys and Robert Giroux

AVON BOOKS
A division of
The Hearst Corporation
959 Eighth Avenue
New York, New York 10019

First Avon Printing, January, 1962
Third Avon Printing, July, 1963
First Avon Library Edition (Fourth Printing) October, 1966

Cover illustration by Saul Lambert

Printed in the U.S.A.

CONTENTS

MEMORIAL DAY

1

ALL the flags were out in front of the houses and stores in Rainbow Center on Memorial Day, as Boyd Mason drove his Buick back from a real-estate trip to Kentucky, and parked on the east corner of Peninsula Drive and Crest Ridge Road, at the side of his sister Alma's house, where he had lived since his wife's death twenty years before.

Slamming his car door shut, he was about to go up the walk to the front porch when he thought he heard a familiar voice reach through his deafness: "Welcome home, Boyd. How you do tramp around the nation at your age!" and turning around he caught sight of Mrs. Barrington, whose two-acre estate directly faced his sister's eight-room house. Boyd put down his canvas bag, in readiness to exchange the time of day with the "old monarch," as everyone called Mrs. Barrington, but when he looked up again he saw his well-wisher already disappearing with a final nod into the leafy regions of her backyard, where English hawthorn, horse chestnut, and azaleas were all in splendid and fragrant bloom, while from the back of her twenty-five-room house Japanese wistaria hung like pear drops from chandeliers.

Turning back again and going up the path to his door, he glanced up gravely at the upper balcony of the house where the huge flag he invariably put up by himself was now flying. He supposed his sister Alma had hired one of the boys from the college to put it up for her, or perhaps she had managed to do it alone. Boyd had a feeling of disappointment, almost guilt, because he had not raised the flag on Memorial Day himself.

Coming inside and setting down his canvas bag again, he greeted his sister drily. One would not have known from her equally undemonstrative salutation that Boyd had been gone, out of the state, for a week.

"Any news?" he shouted in his deaf man's voice.

"A letter from the nephew," Alma cried, and she held the red-white-and-blue envelope out to him.

"A letter from Cliff," Boyd remarked, engrossed in the envelope, his brown eyes aglow. He looked so youthful at that moment, and he was 78.

5

He touched the seal of the letter now, though he knew, of course, that Alma never opened any of his mail. She once nearly did so when their nephew first wrote from Japan. She knew Boyd would not like such interference, though Cliff never told one of them more than he told the other.

Boyd opened the envelope and read the entire letter while still standing balancing on one foot and then the other.

"Well?" Alma asked irritably, while her brother merely smiled, shook his head in amusement, and did nothing to convey what kind of information their nephew's letter contained.

"Oh, Cliff's well," Boyd answered her now. "Read it if you like."

When her look still showed annoyance and a feeling of having been left out, he went on: "He sends his best to you. Says mail call is still the big event of the day at his base."

Alma took the letter almost gingerly, angrily, and went over to Mother's old rocker.

"He writes a good clear hand," Alma said, reading.

"Just a bit childish," Boyd said, low, and when Alma shot him a certain hard critical look, he said, forgetting perhaps that she was reading: "Cliff likes the Pacific. Funny, for I don't think he ever really wanted to leave home, even though he enlisted before he had to, but that was because he felt he should. Wanted to stay put right here in a little town like Rainbow the rest of his natural life. And now look at the distance he's put behind him."

"Yes, I was always the one talked to him about how *I* wanted to travel." Alma looked up from the letter.

"Did you finish reading it?" Boyd wondered.

"If you'll hold your horses——" Alma's voice had a faint scolding edge mixed with the pleasure she so plainly took in handling the nephew's letter.

"Strange how such a young fellow wanted to settle down —and then didn't." He sat down in his own large easy chair. "Well, the army may do him a lot of good, who knows . . .

"Had a word with Mrs. Barrington as I was coming up the walk," Boyd went on, forgetful again that his sister was still reading.

"Yes, I heard her voice."

"The old girl is a spry one at her age. Just think of it— she's near 90."

"She's all of that." Alma looked up as if she, after all, was the authority on age.

"But gad, what a backyard of hers. You have to hand it to her. Those flowering-trees—right at this time of year. No wonder it's a showplace for this part of the country."

"Well, it's all she's ever done—nearly," Alma parenthesized from a critical re-reading of one paragraph of the nephew's letter. "She's had more than two life-times to beautify her property."

Boyd shook his head in amusement and mild disapproval at his sister's critical attitude toward the old monarch.

"Cliff *doesn't* say too much in a letter." Alma moved the stationery in her hand, perhaps under the impression that another sheet still lay concealed beneath the first.

"It's hard to say anything in an overseas letter," Boyd explained. "Also it's better to communicate too little than too much, since he's in service."

"He could tell more," Alma said, folding the delicate thin sheet of paper.

She handed back the letter to Boyd, who put it in his coat pocket.

"I hope you are keeping the letters he sends," Alma told her brother in her still forceful retired-teacher's voice.

"What makes you think I would throw them away?" Boyd inquired.

"I didn't know, of course, what you did with them. But when Cliff comes home, he will probably like to read over his old letters. They will form a kind of diary of what he did."

Boyd snorted.

"I see you don't agree with me," she said tartly.

"You just yourself got through saying he didn't tell anything in his letters. How could they form a diary then, if they tell nothing?"

"I said this particular letter didn't say anything," Alma backtracked awkwardly. "There will be other letters, doubtless, in which he will say more, and such letters will be valuable."

"I had no intention of throwing his letters away," Boyd said in dubious and solemn tones.

"Be sure to hold on to them, then, Boyd," she pontificated. "Or I can keep them, if you want me to."

"I can hold on to them perfectly well, without any help or advice from you." Boyd was emphatic.

"Now I am going to be terribly disappointed if you lose them." She was again the teacher in the classroom. "And I can imagine how Cliff will feel, too."

"I don't think Cliff gives a hollow nut what we do with his letters, and I would be very surprised indeed if he ever asked about them, or wanted to read them, or ever dreamed we would keep them."

"I couldn't disagree more. Everybody likes to think their letters are kept. It's a shame to throw away anybody's letters. Especially those of a young man in service who is at one of the most crucial periods of his life."

"I have no intention whatsoever of throwing away Cliff's letters, and I want you to get that straight in your head."

"Be very careful of them then," Alma said in a soft voice, almost a prayerful whisper of caution, such as she might have used to one of her least understanding students.

"Good God," Boyd cried. "All right, all right. You win." He started to go upstairs.

"Don't be gone for very long now," Alma told him. "Supper is very nearly ready. So don't poke around upstairs for an hour or so, as I don't want to have to shout to you when the meal is ready."

"I will be down as soon as is humanly possible." Boyd glanced indignantly at her. "Hell, a man can have no peace even for a second in this house."

"I am serving supper in five minutes," Alma warned him.

Boyd and Alma had other members in their family, but Cliff was the principal one. The others were married, with children, and lived far off, in California and Canada. They never wrote at all, but sent Christmas cards or Easter greetings when they remembered. And then too Cliff had been partly raised by Boyd and Alma, at least from the age of 14, when he was orphaned by the deaths of both his parents in a plane accident.

During the four or five years he had lived with them in Rainbow Center, Alma was away most of the time teaching school in another town, and Boyd was often gone on his real-estate deals, but for those five years Cliff had been in their house to come home to and to be responsible for, until Korea. Then once he had gone away, they talked of nothing but him.

"Cliff has a great deal of talent," Boyd remarked, seated at the supper table.

"Nobody can deny that," Alma retorted, still a bit cross from their tiff.

"He should make his mark in the world," Boyd said, raising his fork with an expression both of certainty and doubt.

"If we can just let him know we are behind him!" Alma added to his statement, a warning edge coming into her voice.

"Why in thunderation would he ever feel we were not behind him?" Boyd wondered, a bit irritable again.

"All I meant is we must encourage him," Alma explained, somewhat meekly, perhaps almost apologetically for her.

"We must write him encouraging things, and we must encourage him to write to us more often, and tell us more."

"You mean you want him to write to you more often personally?" Boyd inquired.

"I didn't say that," Alma replied.

"I think you meant it, however." He gave her no quarter.

He was eating custard pie, which Alma had taken out of the oven at only five o'clock that very afternoon.

"We must do our best to encourage him," Alma emphasized over his chewing sounds.

"I may not always agree with you about our nephew," Boyd said, finishing the last bite of his custard pie, "but before I disagree with you, I want to compliment you on this pie. Nobody, not even our Mother, could have made a better crust than this."

"What is your point of disagreement?" Alma asked, mildly mollified by his compliment.

"That Cliff is going to turn into a letter-writer," he told her. He pushed back his empty pie plate. "When there's nothing in what he writes now, and never has been."

"Of course there's nothing now," Alma said. "That's the point of everything we have been talking about. We don't encourage him to write good letters. That's what we have got to do, for pity's sake ... He doesn't feel he can write to us."

"We're after all only his uncle and aunt," Boyd said.

"Who else, though, would be interested in Cliff?" Alma asked, perhaps taken aback at the thought.

"Girls maybe. Other young men in service."

"Nonsense. He can't tell *them* the important things. He's got us for that, though perhaps we haven't made it clear to him—that he can depend on us all the way."

She sat back in her chair, having said this, in the guise of digesting her own statement.

"I don't think Cliff is going to write anybody any great shakes of a letter, but if he does happen to, I don't think it will be to us."

"It won't?" Alma said with icy irony.

"That's right. It won't," Boyd said.

"Well, we shall see about that." Alma pushed back her own piece of pie, untasted, from her place.

She put her napkin in the silver ring reserved for it, rose, and went immediately into the kitchen.

Boyd did not take his morning or noon meal with Alma because one dining session a day with her, the evening one, which they denominated *supper*, sufficed in intensity for him.

They were not coffee drinkers, and perhaps for this reason or because of their age, they became sleepy after the meal which usually terminated about 6:15. After Alma dried the dishes, never assisted by Boyd, the two of them dozed intermittently in the sittingroom, frequently still holding before them in sleep the pages of the *Rainbow Sentinel*.

About 8:30 or 9:00, however, they would both wake with a start, and immediately begin talking animatedly, often simultaneously, their newspaper sheets lowered now, so that one would have thought they had been conversing uninterruptedly with one another the entire evening.

On this evening, looking at the social notes in the *Sentinel*, after a lingering glance at obituaries and funerals, Alma exclaimed: "Rainbow has more confounded social activity for such a small place!"

Boyd did not reply. He was perusing the business and financial section of the *Sentinel*, and he rattled its pages, behind which he remained hidden, over the sound of her voice.

"But then at our age," Alma shouted, remembering Boyd's deafness, "one is apt to forget just how much is still going on, even in Rainbow."

Boyd had heard this time, she knew, but he did not volunteer a comment.

"I saw little old Mrs. Van Tassel this afternoon." Alma went on from the events of the town to those of their own immediate neighborhood.

Boyd only said *ahem*. Mrs. Van Tassel, who was even older by a few years than Alma and Boyd and had been a friend of their mother—and for this reason was always addressed by them as Mrs.—lived only a stone's throw across the street.

"Mrs. Van Tassel wanted me to sell my plot of land beyond the wood shed, next to Willard Baker's house."

"Well, I hope you told her you would sell!" Boyd lowered the *Sentinel*.

"No," Alma spoke in measured defiance. "I told her if anything I wanted to buy up more land."

Boyd dropped the newspaper to the floor and stared at his sister in mingled pity and disapproval.

"I don't know why Mrs. Van Tassel wanted a plot of land at her age." Alma turned away from his look. "But I suspect the old girl would like to put up another greenhouse. The one on her own property is not roomy enough for all the flowers she grows."

"I hope, by God, you're not going to get land-poor in *your* old age." Boyd's anger flared up more vividly than she could remember in a long time.

10

"Whatever do you mean by that?"

"You can buy up too much land is what I mean. You've got to be careful about how you invest your money now that you've retired from teaching. And I won't be around forever to advise you. *Don't buy up too much land.*"

He thumped with his hand on the wide wooden arms of his chair. He had assumed more than just his professional manner in dealing with his real-estate clients, and Alma recognized under his advice another unknown source of anger.

When she said nothing, Boyd continued: "Besides, a building of some kind, even a greenhouse, between Willard Baker and here would suit me fine."

"So it boils down to Willard Baker!" Alma said. Then sensing that the significance of her own statement perhaps escaped her, she added: "What on earth can you have against poor Willard? We've known him, for pity's sake, since he was a boy."

"Since he was a boy," he snorted. Looking at her with his clear straight gaze he said, "Willard's crowding fifty if he's a minute."

Boyd had picked up the newspaper again, but he did not cover himself with it immediately, for they had touched on a subject which did not let go of him too easily.

"Your trouble, Alma," he went on, "is you've been gone too long. You mentioned a bit further back how much was going on in Rainbow now. It's not what's going on now you've missed out on as much as what went on when you weren't here at all . . ."

"Oh, that's what everybody has always said. I've been gone from the town too long to know this, remember that, to have heard this scandal or been in on that. The fact that I've taught the fifth grade all my life makes everybody think I wouldn't understand what goes on in people's houses in any case."

Boyd smiled sardonically and with a certain fulsome satisfaction. "Now about Willard Baker," he lectured her gravely. "He's changed a darned sight since he was a boy, don't forget. And he's changed some again in the past ten years."

Alma waited, pursing her mouth in disbelief.

"For one thing old Willard's been keeping company with a . . . bad penny, name of Vernon Miller—young enough to be his son. They go it some nights pretty bad. Women from out of town over there drinking, and that sort of thing every week-end. They carry on till morning."

Alma refused to look distressed or concerned.

"Your bedroom don't face his side of the house," Boyd finished his accusation with vehemence.

11

"We can move your bedroom downstairs where you don't face Willard at all," she retorted.

She cleared her throat, which he interpreted as a sign from her to drop the subject of Willard Baker, but when Boyd said nothing more at all, frowning at his high, refulgently polished shoes, it was Alma who went on:

"Of course, like Mother, I'd like to have the house always surrounded by my own property . . . And in any case I don't see how a small greenhouse—one Mrs. Van Tassel would build, at any rate—would shut off anything . . . *undesirable.*"

Boyd sensed, however, that she was a bit surprised at his anger over Willard Baker, for as Alma was never tired of harping, the Bakers were one of the few "front" families in town.

When Boyd preserved his silence, she continued: "If the business part of town continues to move down here, we will be protected against office buildings and the like springing up around us, for the first thing a business concern would buy up would be a greenhouse, especially if Mrs. Van Tassel were the owner!"

"If the business part of town, as you put it, moves down here, there will be nothing you or I, Mrs. Van Tassel, God Almighty, or even Mrs. Barrington can do about it. They will buy up everything."

"Not until they have done battle with me," Alma said.

Boyd smiled his wry pitying smile.

"Well," he pretended to dismiss the subject, "perhaps you are right in buying up plots of ground, or keeping what you have . . . Who can advise in times like the present?"

"I would like to be surrounded *always* by my own property," Alma summarized her own feeling again. "But for pity's sake," she suddenly levelled her attack, "I wish you wouldn't be so mysterious about Willard Baker. If there's something I should know about him, for heaven's sake tell me, and don't imply that there's more to his character than I could ever hope to understand."

"Mysterious, hell," Boyd thundered. "What more is there to tell you about him than I've told, for God's sake? All I know about him is what everybody but evidently you knows about him. He drinks and carouses and gambles."

"Well, Willard Baker or no Willard Baker, I have the right to dispose of my own property as I see fit," she replied firmly to his unexpected warmth.

The house and land were hers, of course, but what they had touched on, she saw, was not only Willard Baker, but what everybody she knew seemed now always to be touch-

12

ing on with regard to her—the larger area of her ignorance about the town and, as Boyd sometimes bore home to her with a bluntness which was almost brutality, her ignorance about people and life.

When Boyd had retired, Alma beat her eternal path to the kitchen, which faced directly—though it was a good half-block away separated from her by a field of soft green perfectly cared-for grass—the large sprawling 19th-century house of Willard Baker, whose family, her lips could never stop repeating, had been along with Mrs. Barrington's one of the oldest and most respected in that part of the country.

Willard had always been, Alma could now remember, a kind of ne'er-do-well, changing jobs frequently, or being out of work entirely and sitting home enjoying his mother's cooking. Then there had been the period in his life when he had "arrived" and had been a private detective in Chicago, to the amusement of the older families in town. But why Boyd could get angry over Willard—well.

She supposed that in the end it had to do with some quarrel over real estate and money, and not with "loose living" at all, for real estate was where Boyd's feelings were deepest, she was sure, and where everything for him always finally came to rest. Willard had never been a model of business acumen and would not be Boyd's kind of man.

Not wanting to go to bed yet, Alma remained gazing out the kitchen window. Willard had passed completely out of her thoughts when, looking out the north window absentmindedly, she caught sight of the Baker house, which glowed faintly in the moonlight.

A shaft of light at that moment illuminated, in its old position in the yard, a wooden plaque, never removed, which still read

THE DOCTORS
BAKER

Alma nodded, remembering.

Willard's father and his younger brother Joe had been physicians and surgeons of note in the town, and in the state. They had practised medicine together in rooms easily set apart for that purpose in so large a house; but now it was occupied only by Willard.

The tragedy in the Baker family had been simple and terrible and complete. Doctor Joe, as everyone addressed him, who had always been a town model for character, uprightness and brains—the direct opposite of Willard in everything—became involved in what amounted to a virtual public scandal, a love-affair with a young married woman in Cincinnati. In the disgrace which followed, and in the falling off of both doctors' practice, Joe, everybody was convinced, had turned to drugs; then, hopelessly addicted, one bright June day in his consulting room before the eyes of a young boy whom he was treating for a cut finger, he shot himself to death. Dr. Baker senior died of a heart attack a week or so later. The mother, whose sun rose and set in Doctor Joe, lingered on a year later in a condition which mercifully, perhaps, allowed her to mistake Willard for his younger and favored brother. She died, Willard's hand in hers, believing that his touch was that of her beloved Doctor Joe.

Willard drank, as Boyd had complained, and lived at the race track, brought women and suspicious-looking men to the house over Sundays, and the rest of the week passed much of his time alone with his bottle and his long cigars, taking repeated but very short strolls which had no particular direction and seemingly no purpose except to get him out of the house.

Drawing the shade quickly, Alma closed from view the plaque bearing the doctors' names, and made her way up to her own bedroom for sleeplessness or sleep.

THE NEIGHBORS

2

ALMA and Boyd's arguments about the content or lack of content of Cliff's letters came to an unexpected end, so unexpected and quiet in its suddenness that it left behind for a while no emotion which could be easily observed and, like Cliff's letter, almost assumed the appearance of a blank.

Early one June morning when a summer thundershower, followed by hail and sleet, suddenly turned back the clock to an icy spring, and Alma hugged the house to herself, the telegram from Washington arrived. For some reason it was addressed to her rather than, as had always been the case in the past, to Boyd.

The telegram had several misspellings caused (Alma was instantly sure) by the local Rainbow office. It simply stated that Cliff was missing in action, after having been wounded a week earlier in Korea.

The casual and empty wording of the message for a moment did not convey to her the dreadfulness of the import —and perhaps did not for a long time to come. Again, like Cliff's letters, the "content" did not quite come through, and she was left with the impression that a more complete message would soon be on its way.

As in certain fatal accidents where the injured person may never feel anything at all until the very last moment, Alma went about the entire day with her work and her gift shop, not taking in the exact weight of the telegram. Of course *missing*, she told herself each hour of the day, was not by any means the same as *will not return*.

Only the expression on Boyd's face after he returned from the real-estate office that evening for supper shattered the specious security the day had bestowed on her.

They never mentioned the word *dead* from that moment. Alma herself never even considered—at least in words—that Cliff had died. Whatever Boyd may have thought, the look on his sister's face prevented him from even hinting it by expression or word, but in her case, part of her character, one might say, changed from her looking at her brother's face that evening.

For Alma, from that moment on, Cliff was more alive

than ever, and his homecoming a future actuality which must crown all her hopes and longings.

The letters from Cliff once stopped, with their paltry information and insipid leave-takings (*your devoted nephew, Cliff*), the aunt and uncle now might have been said to apostrophize the soldier, as one would a saint, for while before there had been little to say about him or his letters,, there was now almost less than nothing. Yet they talked, and spoke his name.

For some time after Cliff had been reported missing, Alma had allowed Boyd the freedom to say that *he didn't know, just didn't know*, until one evening, at the beginning of summer, putting down the *Sentinel*, she said with great sternness and force:

"I don't know why in heaven's name you keep saying *you don't know* when it is perfectly clear that you think he won't return."

"That's not what I think at all. Not by a long shot," he replied, both wounded and incensed. "As usual, you're jumping to conclusions before you see the evidence."

"I *know* he'll be back" she cried, in the same tones she employed in her political and religious arguments.

"I know you do," Boyd said in his most conciliatory manner, placing the argument now likewise in the arena of the historical and objective. "But when I say I don't *know*, I mean just that."

"Fiddle," she said with real anger.

"I don't know, Alma," he told her, and he shook the pages of the *Sentinel*.

"You have a feeling one way or another. Everybody does."

"How like a woman," he shook his head.

"You have your own feeling, which is stronger in one direction or another, and being a man or woman has nothing to do with it. Everybody who thinks or feels knows what he thinks or feels about someone's being missing or not missing, going to return or not going to return."

"All right, all right," Boyd bent under her attack.

"I know you think Cliff's not coming back," Alma said, and her voice broke.

He had not seen Alma cry for too many years to remember. He did not know whether she could. However, at this moment for the first time in recent memory, he saw her come very close to breaking.

"I hope against hope is all," Boyd finally said in a subdued reverent voice.

"If it's the best you can do!" Alma's voice was hard and clear again.

She rose and went upstairs without her usual dispassion-ate *goodnight*.

Sometimes, after they had done battle together, as they had tonight, he would hear her later furiously breaking wind in her bedroom, and since she was such a proper fastidious person, he wondered whether she went to her bedroom at such times for the reason that she knew she was going to break wind, or whether she broke wind as an aftermath of their disputes together.

Once she had left the room, he leafed through the *Sentinel* a few more times, skimming the results of the State College's baseball victories, perusing the notices of new lots opening up on Sugar Ridge, turned the radio on for a moment to get the weather report, stuck his nose out the door to test the temperature, then went to his own bedroom where he would toss and turn for an hour or two in his four-poster before drifting off into a restless old man's sleep.

In her room, too, Alma was restless, and sometimes mut-tered aloud about Boyd's insensitivity and blindness. A brother like him, or any brother, for that matter, left so much to be desired.

The letters from Cliff having stopped, the postman now seldom ever crossed over to their side of Peninsula Drive.

Alma had felt the Government would be duty-bound to write a long letter at regular intervals concerning Cliff, a communiqué sort of thing, complicated and detailed, but aside from one short and nearly unintelligible paragraph from a colonel whose name had been signed by his male secretary, there had been nothing at all from that quarter.

At 9:00 each morning, nonetheless, Alma went to the front door and waited unostentatiously in the shadow of the screen door as the postman made his rounds. Watching him like this each day brought her slowly, as in a lesson to a retarded pupil, to a kind of inventory of who was left and who was dead in her immediate neighborhood, for de-spite her long absence from Rainbow Center, the neighbors here had been hers for life.

To her mortification, she saw that the postman almost always had a letter for each house on the block but hers. (Boyd would, of course, insist on getting his personal mail at his real-estate office.)

Mrs. Barrington, as might be expected, received the great-est volume of mail of anybody in town and the most spe-cial attention from the post office. In the past the neighbors used to say that Mrs. B. should have her own private postal service owing to the bulk of letters she received. And Alma

17

felt a certain annoyance over the old monarch's frequent gratuities to the postman and her occasionally inviting him in for "refreshments"—a most questionable practice, in Alma's opinion.

"Now who on earth writes Clara Himbaugh that many letters!" Alma cried one morning when she saw the postman carrying a huge sheaf of mail to the house directly adjoining that of Willard Baker.

Then Alma remembered that Clara, of course, had been a Christian Science practitioner since the days of her own mother, and the bulk of the mail must have to do, she saw at once, with Clara's proselytes, and the practising of her religion.

Alma remembered back four or five years ago when Clara had had all her teeth pulled without allowing the dentist to give her an anesthetic. After the extraction, Clara had disappeared for a few days. Alma had finally gone to the Scientist's house, and after a futile ten minutes of knocking at the screen door which had roused Willard Baker next door from his late morning snooze, she entered Clara's house unannounced. She found the latter in a semi-conscious and perhaps delirious state, recognizing nothing and nobody, and making sounds which resembled those of a puppy. Alma brought her some hot bouillon, and then summoned a physician, who gave her an injection.

Whether Clara ever knew that Alma had summoned a physician in direct contradiction of her religious beliefs, nobody knew. But Clara had always shown her appreciation of Alma's interest in her, even when sometimes they had long—and on Alma's side—almost bitter arguments about Christian Science.

"You've simply got to give up this faith of yours or it's going to kill you," Alma had told Clara a few days after the near-tragedy of the dental extraction.

Clara said nothing.

"The dentist should have refused to do such a thing to you in the first place, faith or no faith. And above all, why on earth did you have your teeth pulled? Wasn't Science strong enough to allow you to forget about them too?"

"I will not quarrel with you, Alma, because you are not trying to understand."

"Had it not been for me, you would have died," Alma replied, with her characteristic bluntness concerning other people's weakness. "What do you say to that?"

Clara merely smiled her sweet understanding smile, and patted the arms of the chair in which she was sitting comfortably in her convalescence.

Now that Cliff was missing, the tables were to a degree,

if not entirely, turned. It was Clara who now, ever so imperceptibly, talked down to Alma. Once, only a few days before, after a heated argument on Alma's part, Clara had said after a long pause:

"Science could help *you*, Alma."

Alma gave Clara a look of almost imperial contradiction coupled with a command for silence. Recovering some of her old assurance, Alma said: "There's nothing wrong with me, Clara, and you know it."

"I'm afraid there's something wrong with us all," Clara contradicted.

Alma was not able to get the word *fiddle* out when Clara was already on her way with: "If you had something to cling to, you wouldn't have grasped as you're doing at Cliff's memory, I mean."

The look on Alma's face brought Clara up short and sharp and she said no more for a moment, but then seeing that she had gone this far, Clara continued: "All I mean is, Alma dear, if you had the attitude of Science toward those passed over . . . if you could give up your way of thinking about the absent. . . . "

"I have never for a moment considered the thought that Cliff is dead," Alma said in a voice which was unrecognizable to both of them, and much lower in tone now than that of a man's.

"My dear, I didn't mean—" Clara saw the danger for both of them.

"I believe that Cliff is alive and will come home," Alma pronounced in a firm overloud voice which certainly must have reached Willard Baker, for he came out on the porch and looked in the direction of Clara's.

"Everything is all right with Cliff," Clara said positively now.

"I know you think he is dead," Alma accused her suddenly, and her capacity to attack had calmed some of her own emotion.

"My dear child!" Clara protested in her most human tones. "*I*, of all people!" She appealed to something larger than themselves, but she saw at once Alma recognized neither the appeal nor the meaning.

"I can read people's expressions. A child, after all, can. And I knew the day he was reported missing and you came over to my place to give your condolences that you believed him dead, or passed over, or whatever term you use."

Alma followed her statement by a short rather sour laugh. She straightened a brooch on her breast which had belonged to her mother, and which she had begun to wear only after retiring from the teaching profession.

Clara, however, was already speaking in her hushed but strong "reader's" tones: "Alma, there is no death. How could I believe, therefore, that Cliff was dead? And I hesitate, my dear, even to employ these words. I only use them because of your attitude."

"*My* attitude?" Alma shook her head. "You believe that he has been called away then, since you don't like the word the rest of the human race has been perfectly satisfied to use with regard to what happens to every last one of us."

"I feel Cliff is right here with us, and I feel it every time I think of him," Clara Himbaugh said.

Alma paused over this. She was not a religious woman, and she was not a woman who liked to hear the great sentiments discussed and paraded, but there was something about Clara's statement which touched her. She bowed her head for a moment. Then beginning to rock again in her chair, she merely said, "Of course he is."

"I am sorry if we have seemed to disagree," Clara Himbaugh brought out, all her sweetness and odorless exertion in evidence again.

Alma shook her head gently. "You are talking about one thing, and I am talking about another," she explained to the Scientist. "You believe Cliff will never come back in the flesh, and that he has been called off to some mansion. I don't believe in any mansion for the dead, and I believe Cliff will be home . . . in *person*."

"I do, too, Alma!" Clara expostulated. "I have always believed that. I believe it with all my heart and mind. You must believe that I believe. Do not doubt me."

"Very well, Clara," Alma gave a bit. "But the day you came here after the Government announced his being missing, your face belied what you have just now said to me."

"I was uncertain and shaken," Clara accepted the charge. "I'm afraid I was not at my best that day."

"We won't harp on it, Clara, my dear," Alma smiled gravely.

"Cliff *will* be . . ."

"No more, Clara!"

". . . back!" Clara finished.

"Have you heard about Mrs. Van Tassel's new woman boarder?" Alma underscored the change in subject by the hardness and loudness of her voice.

"The lady with the cane?"

Alma nodded.

"Just a word or two got to me," Clara admitted, and suddenly she sniggered like a small girl in Sunday school.

"It's too bad for dear old Mrs. Van Tassel," Alma ignored Clara's outburst. "She's afraid to take college boys for roomers, and I don't blame her for that, but taking in an unmarried woman—though in this case a widow—can be almost as risky, and in a way, more bother."

Clara nodded.

Alma had reference to Mrs. Minnie Clyde Hawke, who had been left a widow a year or so ago. Shortly after her husband's funeral—she had slipped, she said, on the treacherous gravel-path in Naple Grove Cemetery—she had taken to carrying a cane. In the last month or so she had come asking to rent Mrs. Van Tassel's large front room on the pretext that memories would no longer let her live in her own beautiful fifteen-room house. A week or so ago, Mrs. Van Tassel had granted Mrs. Hawke's request and the widow had shut up her house and moved in.

Not many days later when she entered Mrs. Hawke's room early one evening to tidy up, under the impression that her new boarder had gone out, what was Mrs. Van Tassel's surprise therefore to find Mrs. Hawke's cane lying in two pieces on the writing-table, with a brandy flask—which had ostensibly come out of the hollow leg of the cane—opened and half-consumed. Mrs. Hawke herself in a soiled wrapper was drinking out of one of Mrs. Van Tassel's nicest cut-glass tumblers from the china closet downstairs.

"I'm so sorry, Mrs. Hawke," little Mrs. Van Tassel had babbled. "I was entirely under the impression you had gone out."

Alma said she would not repeat what Mrs. Hawke had said in reply. "Of course," Alma hastened to say, under the crushed and wounded expression of Clara Himbaugh's eyes, "of course, she was under the influence or she would have never said such a thing to an old lady like Mrs. V. T. She had been closeted in there drinking, evidently, all the afternoon."

Clara Himbaugh closed her eyes gently, and smiled benignantly. She never commented on such things one way or another, but seemed, while attentive to such stories (she never forbade gossip in her presence) to act like one immersed in prayer.

Suddenly, however, Clara inquired:

"Will Mrs. Hawke continue to live with Mrs. Van Tassel?"

"Mrs. V. T. is not sure, I gather from something she said to me the other day. She does not want to ask Mrs. Hawke to leave. It would cause more talk, for one thing. At the same time, it is plainly a medical case. Alcoholism, you know, in the last stages."

21

Clara gave a brief sad nod.

"Mrs. Hawke has been everywhere with that new cane. The movies, church, the lodge, tea parties, even a few recent funerals. She can't be without it, and there isn't any evidence she ever slipped at the cemetery, you know."

"And all this time her beautiful fifteen-room house is shut up and empty," Clara lamented.

Alma assented to this expression of regret with a grave bow, and then rose to take her leave.

Clara also stood up, while inquiring, "Is Boyd up and about as usual?"

"Boyd still goes down to his real-estate office every day," Alma replied somewhat drily.

"Isn't it glorious at his age!" Clara cried with complete conviction, and in a voice which Alma thought a bit too robust and cheery for the commonplaceness of the thought.

"You dare not let down, Clara," Alma explained.

Clara opened the screen door for her visitor. Then as they hugged one another gently goodbye on the porch, Clara cried impulsively: "You have so many beautiful memories of Cliff, Alma dear . . . Why don't you put them all down—in a kind of *book!*"

The sudden expression of such an idea was so unexpected that almost unconsciously Alma pushed the Scientist out of her embrace.

"It's not quite time for a *memorial*, Clara," Alma said, wide-eyed, and a bit pale. Her severity, however, embarrassed both of them.

"That wasn't quite my meaning, Alma dear," Clara's voice followed the nephew's aunt down the walk, too soft for the latter to hear.

The word *memorial*, however, stuck in Alma's mind like a melody she had heard unwillingly and even more unwillingly remembered.

To drive out its sound and meaning, she babbled at the supper table that evening, broaching the subject of Mrs. Hawke and her cane with the hollow leg, but Boyd refused to listen, explaining that he had never been interested in that kind of talk when he was a young man, and now that he was old he had even less intention of giving it an ear.

Putting down her fork, Alma said, "I don't think what happens to a friend and neighbor can be construed as just talk. If you had any kind of community feeling, you would *care* what happens to little Mrs. Van Tassel . . . She's terribly worried about having Mrs. Hawke on her hands."

"Let her tell Mrs. Hawke to leave then," Boyd replied, impassive.

"Easier said than done!" Alma said, getting up to serve the dessert.

"I'll go over and have a talk with Mrs. Van Tassel," Boyd was conciliatory when Alma returned to the dining table with the hot custard pie.

"You'll do nothing of the kind," Alma told him, putting his pie plate down with a vigorous thump before him.

"I think I may," Boyd said, cutting almost half of his serving of pie in two and eating this still-steaming half immediately.

He chewed loudly, with his mouth open, so that if one sat at the right angle one could see his tongue laden with custard and crust, churning implacably. He had never learned to close his mouth when he ate, and he ate most audibly. Alma usually turned away when he chewed, but she stared at him now, as if to take in the full unsightliness of his table etiquette and, armed with this vision, be even firmer with him in the future.

"For years, possibly," Alma began, as he finished the custard pie, "for months now, Mrs. Clyde Hawke has been deceiving everybody with her cane. No one, so far as I know, ever suspected she drank heavily. They thought it was high blood pressure which made her giddy. Yet her cane was nonetheless a source of puzzlement."

"An affectation, the merchants downtown thought." Boyd wiped his mouth on his napkin, still chewing, his eyes not quite focused in the pleasure of digestion.

"No one could call it affectation now," Alma intoned, removing a few dishes from the table.

"Aren't you eating any pie?" Boyd inquired, staring at her, a bit sheepish perhaps that he had made away with his before she had even begun.

"I may have a bite later in the kitchen," Alma's voice softened a bit at his inquiry.

"You let the neighbors upset you," Boyd told her.

"I don't like to think of old Mrs. Van Tassel being in the same house with a crazy spoiled drinking woman," Alma said from the inner recesses of the kitchen.

Boyd had not heard her, and he was by now already in the front room ensconced in his arm chair, reading the *Sentinel*.

"God, you can't look after everybody," he mumbled.

"What's that you say?" Alma shouted from the kitchen. Usually she ignored his mutterings in the front room, but she did not like the way he showed such indifference to Mrs. Van Tassel's problem this evening.

"Didn't say a thing!" Boyd shouted when she repeated her question.

"There's a pretty big gulf separating gossip from concern about one's neighbors," she informed him, stepping briefly into the front room in deference to his deafness.

"All right, I stand corrected," Boyd avoided further conflict so soon after supper.

"Nothing is being exaggerated or misstated in my discussion of what is going on at Mrs. Van Tassel's."

"I'm aware of that," Boyd shook the pages of the *Sentinel*.

"I'm very much concerned about the situation," Alma said, retreating again into the kitchen. She splashed her hands around in the suds of the dish-pan. "No one can tell what a spoiled rich woman like Mrs. Hawke may do, in any case." She spoke so softly that her voice barely reached him behind the pages of the newspaper.

Almost the only person Alma could talk to in the neighborhood, or indeed all of Rainbow Center, and the only woman perhaps she had anything in common with was the college instructor in beginners' French, Faye Laird, whom townspeople continued to refer to as *Mrs. Laird's daughter*.

Faye and her mother lived catty-cornered across the street from Alma's and Boyd's, adjoining Mrs. Van Tassel's house, and directly across the street from the houses of Willard Baker and Clara Himbaugh.

Faye had taught at the State College for nearly half her life, although she was still under 45. She came home from her classes early each afternoon (college teaching did give her a certain freedom, unlike the fifth grade, she often told Alma) to care for her mother, who was bedridden most of the time now, and could no longer remember people's names, and. sometimes did not recognize her own daughter.

The day Alma had gone over to tell Faye about Cliff's being reported missing, Mrs. Laird had called down from the upstairs to demand what the two women were doing in her living room.

"Mother, it's only your own little Faye, and Alma Mason," the daughter had replied in a kind of mortified baby-talk.

"Faye!" Mrs. Laird had snorted. "Faye eloped years ago with a low-down chiseller from the First National Bank. Don't talk to me about my own daughter . . ."

Mrs. Laird referred to the time nearly thirty years ago when Faye, only 16, was to have married the bank president's son, Bob Phillips. Mrs. Laird, having heard some talk about the young man's private life in Cincinnati, had put her foot down. The engaged couple kept putting off their wedding day (Mrs. Laird would not allow an open rupture) and then, finally, their engagement and wedding were indefinitely postponed and never spoken of again. Young Phillips went to Los Angeles after a time, and became a prominent business and social success there. He never returned to Rainbow Center again except to attend his father's funeral.

Faye seemed to have no bitterness against her mother's having spoiled her chances of marriage. Faye had always been an extremely small girl, and at the age of 25 looked only 14. Now, over 40, she looked neither young nor old, middle-aged or mature. There was something of the midget in her face, not wrinkled enough for a woman of 40, and too worn for that of a child.

Alma felt that Faye almost enjoyed her mother's long illness, and her treatment of her mother resembled that bestowed on a favorite child. Faye spent long hours with the old woman, singing to her, and talking to her in a language and vocabulary part of which was understandable only between themselves.

Boyd always shook his head when he heard more "news" from Alma about Faye and Mrs. Laird. He was of the solidified opinion that Mrs. Laird had been a selfish and overbearing mother, and that Faye had paid a terrible price for her devotion. Boyd repeatedly prophesied that when Mrs. Laird died, Faye would face the supreme crisis of her life, and might even have a breakdown and become as helpless as her mother.

"She will manage to keep busy at something," Alma contradicted Boyd's statement with a good deal of warmth.

After she had engaged in these discussions with Boyd about Faye, Alma often sat thinking that her own mother had occupied a good deal of *her* life. However, Alma had finally left her mother and gone away to teach school in a neighboring state, and after all the worry and the care and the financial burden, which Boyd did not share, her mother had died, leaving her, until the days of Cliff, with emptiness and unspent energy.

Then when Boyd's wife, Netta, had died, Boyd came to live with her, and finally Alma retired from teaching to take up the remainder of her life in Rainbow Center.

Sometimes she and Boyd were mistaken by the young, or those who had not known them earlier, for man and wife, a mistake which pleased neither of them.

Now like her mother before her, Alma rocked a good deal in the chair, and looked out the window which faced, from one angle or another, the houses of Faye Laird,

Willard Baker, Clara Himbaugh, and Mrs. Van Tassel. She kept a replenished store of nuts for the squirrels, which were numerous in the neighborhood, and she grew a number of unusual plants and flowers indoors.

Her main occupation after retiring was to have been her gift shop. She gave more worry to it than any other kind of attention. Most of the time now she thought about people—not, she was sure, with the kind of curiosity which can only be appeased by gossip, but with a growing sense of mystery and unease.

And always in the background now there was the presence of Cliff. She could not understand how, merely by reason of his having put on Uncle Sam's clothes, he could go to that faraway Pacific place and never return.

AN ODOR OF KETCHUP

3

IN July, the wagons and trucks with the red juicy ripened fruit were already on their route to the ketchup factory, and a few days later one smelled the first intense high odor of mingled tomatoes, spices, and sugar.

For the first few days of the ketchup "season," Alma was invariably ill. Fortunately, the smell lasted only a few weeks at the most—but those weeks made up the summer. At the first frost, with doors and windows closed, the trees dropping their leaves, one could forget about ketchup and the ketchup factory until another year.

This summer, with the heat and the heavy burning fruit attar everywhere, Alma remembered that Cliff too had disliked the smell of the cooking tomatoes. One July, when she had for once refused to teach summer school, she and Cliff had spent more than the usual amount of time together. One afternoon, for a solid hour, while playing checkers together, they had taken turns complaining vociferously against the ketchup factory.

"It's bread and butter to the people connected with the industry," Boyd reminded them soberly. "This whole town would be broke without ketchup." And he went on to remind them that even in the darkest days of the depression, the ketchup factory had kept going.

"Can openers and ketchup continued to sell during the worst years of unemployment," Boyd concluded.

And now, Alma thought, remembering her conversations with Cliff and sniffing the odor that announced summer in Rainbow Center, Cliff no longer existed, except for the "missing" in front of his name.

Since Alma had retired from teaching and no longer spent most of her day with children, she had become increasingly dissatisfied with her understanding and knowledge of adult problems and lives. She did not understand, she supposed, as she had heard her mother say many years before, "the main things about life," and she had come to attribute this to her being an old-maid schoolteacher.

But with Cliff "missing," and with merely a tepid interest in her gift shop, she found herself left only with adult problems—her neighbors'. There was very little else to think about but Minnie Clyde Hawke's cane, Willard Baker's intemperance, and Mrs. Laird's having spoiled her daughter Faye's chances.

In the sudden engulfing emptiness of her life, the word *memorial* which had escaped either from her own mouth or Clara Himbaugh's (she was no longer certain which) continued to stay with her, as persistent as the odor of the ketchup. She hated the tone, the sound, the meaning of *memorial* as much as she did that of the ketchup, and the two, odor and word, were an exacerbation in her mind.

"You could write down everything you know about him." She thought she heard Clara's dulcet words coming to her over the wave of cooking sweet tomatoes. "You could tell what Cliff did and accomplished. Others have done it before you."

"But of course Cliff will be back," Alma said aloud. "Memorials are for those who won't!"

The sound of her own voice broke her revery, and presented her with her own small but peculiar and real dilemma. Outside of her preoccupation with the neighbors and her inexact attention to the gift shop, she was uneasily aware now that many of her hours were spent in a dim dream-like reshaping of Cliff's life, and her reveries themselves were often a silent commemoration of his brief career.

She was glad she had that one photograph of him, and even gladder, often, that she had all his letters. To many people, like Boyd, the letters said nothing. It was exactly in the little they said that Alma read the much that was there. It was in Cliff's omissions that she saw his life.

Boyd, of course, had cared for Cliff deeply in his way, as a man without sons can sometimes care, but she was sure Cliff did not occupy the same area of consciousness as he did with her. There was hardly an hour in Alma's waking life when she did not think of Cliff. In this way, he had taken the place of her mother.

Even when Cliff had been a small boy and his parents were still living, he had occupied a peculiarly meaningful and at the same time obscure room in her heart. She had not understood it, but after he had been reported missing, she came for the first time to acknowledge to herself, if not to others, the fundamental, if indefinable, importance he had assumed in her life, and she was often sure that it was she and not Boyd who felt Cliff would never come back.

That was, perhaps, why she was so indignant that Boyd

was non-committal about Cliff's being "missing" or—something else. Boyd, as the man of the house, should tell her one way or another: was Cliff coming home or wasn't he? But Boyd had also a man's vague, persistent, objective deferred opinion, which she both respected and despised.

Today Boyd had returned unexpectedly early from his real-estate office and his sudden entrance startled her from her revery.

"What are you upset about now?" Boyd cried, taken aback at the enigmatic expression on her face.

"I beg your pardon." Alma flushed with anger, as if he had opened the door of her dressing-room. "A person can't even wear a normal expression of concentration in this house without being criticized for it."

But her hands, as well as the expression she had worn, were too eloquent of emptiness. She stood up at once and walked over to the deal table where she had left a linen tablecloth that needed stitching.

"Confound it," Boyd scolded. "I hope you're not worrying your head off about Mrs. Van Tassel and her boarder. She's not worth it."

"Who's not worth it?" Alma pretended anger now, but she smiled, too, with some relief then, for he was, as usual, off the track, so far as she herself was concerned.

"Neither of them cussed females, Minnie Hawke or Mrs. Van Tassel herself—getting you upset like this . . ."

Alma sat down with the table cloth and explored its surface by touching it gently with her needle.

"There's no need for Mrs. Van Tassel to take boarders," Boyd returned to the subject almost compulsively.

"Mrs. Hawke is not a *boarder*," Alma took up the discussion with mechanical welcome. "She merely rents the big front room that faces us. She takes all her meals at the *Candle Glow*."

"Mrs. Van Tassel always turned up her nose at renting her rooms to office girls, or to a college boy even—who would have been some help and protection to her." Boyd repeated a speech he had already made to Alma a score of times, but she listened as attentively now as if he had come home from the office expressly to tell her some important story. "In a way I'm glad she got stuck with this old girl she thought would be such a feather in her cap living with her: 'Minnie Clyde Hawke is staying with me.' I can still hear her chirping all over the neighborhood, trying to impress people because she thought Minnie was 'somebody' . . . And now she turns out to be a boozer."

"Oh, for pity's sake," Alma complained, laughing in spite of herself, and threatening to drop her linen table cloth.

29

Then expanding her nostrils, she said, "I so *loathe* that smell."

Boyd frowned at her.

"What would you say if I wrote a short account of Cliff's career?" she remarked to Boyd a day or so later.

"Who gave you that idea?" He put down the new issue of the *National Geographic*.

"Oh, it's not going to be a *memorial*, if that's what you're thinking," she snapped, but without her usual astringent tone.

"Well, I should hope not," he replied, and there was a kind of embarrassment in his manner.

"Memorial was Clara Himbaugh's term for it, I'm afraid," Alma said, and she was suddenly surprised at her own coyness. She wanted Boyd to draw her out.

"That's news, I must say," Boyd chuckled from his new height. "Getting your ideas from Clara Himbaugh, I mean." He did not spare her his condescension.

"I didn't say anything about the idea coming from her," she said weakly. She recognized at once her own untruth, and at the thought it was Clara who had suggested an idea she had latched on to with such possessive hold, she blushed.

"Well, memorial is a hell of a term for it, if you ask me." Boyd returned to the *Geographic*.

"It was just a thought!" she said impatiently, getting up.

"What's wrong with your gift shop?" he came back to this. "The three or four years before you retired that was all you talked about. Said you would welcome the day when you could devote yourself to it."

"Oh, I suppose the location's wrong," she accepted his criticism today with humbleness and equanimity. "Or it's me maybe . . . I'll come to it, though," she came back with a bit more of her former vigor. "I should travel too, I suppose, to really find things that people want from a shop like mine."

"Well, I don't know what in thunderation you'd put in your memorial to Cliff," he said as she began to leave the room.

She waited for a moment.

"It would be a kind of family thing," she said softly.

"I see," he said, respectful of her tone.

He did not agree with her, she saw, and with a certain anger she recognized the pity he felt for her. It meant, of course, that if he did not encourage her exactly in writing the memorial—and there the name stuck!—he would go

30

along with her "whim" as he had in the matter of the gift shop. For Boyd always opposed her up to a point. Then he gave in with his usual condescension, indifference, pity, or amusement, depending on the circumstance and on his own point of view at the time.

Coming into the room again later, she showed him a huge rather ugly black notebook stamped RECORDS, which she said she would use as a "beginning" for what she might write about Cliff.

"A kind of record just for us," she explained, but her voice was not loud enough this time to reach through his deafness, and it never occurred to him that it would be for anybody but herself.

The front part of the downstairs was still divided into two large rooms. The west room, which in the days before they had installed a furnace was usually closed off, was the least used, and the east room which faced Mrs. Van Tassel's and the Lairds' was the one Alma and Boyd kept as their living room. But now that she had the "record" book, she began sitting in the west room at a large walnut desk which had been her father's and which in the past nobody had employed except Boyd, from time to time, when he wished to talk privately with a real-estate client, or go through ancient tax notices.

But whether it was the business and legal appearance of the "record" book and its pages, or something deeper she dared not consider, she wrote nothing those first few days, but she remembered more in that time than she had perhaps in her entire previous life, and in remembering she found a quiet and concentrated something which surprised her. There had been four nephews, and all of them had seen military service, but the three who returned— Junie, Gabe, and Johnson—had married and gone West. They seldom wrote or sent gifts and remembrances, and in the end, Alma knew, it was they who were actually "missing."

Although Alma had often had misgivings about Cliff's ability and even his character—the other three nephews had always seemed much more successful and "adjusted" in everything they did—he alone had been her favorite from the beginning, and phenomenon of phenomenons, Boyd's, for on every other subject under the sun she and Boyd had disagreed except on this one: in Cliff's case they were in total agreement, hopeless unanimity: Cliff had something, they were sure.

It was hard, though, to know what Cliff *had,* though Alma was more sure now than ever that he had it. The photograph of him in the east living room seemed almost retouched. It made him look almost pretty in that pose, and Cliff had not been even very good-looking. But he possessed that astonishing fresh look, as if he had just come out of a forest, perhaps, or even a pond, still dripping a little from his bath.

The great thing about Cliff was that he had been content to sit with old people, to talk to them as though no gulf or barrier of age existed and to be at ease with them. Even his laugh when he was with them was as natural and unselfconscious as it was with his own contemporaries. He had taken no more note of the passing of time with them than they had: the other nephews excused themselves after ten minutes of conversation. With Cliff the minutes passed easily into hours as he chatted with Boyd and Alma, and they had never forgotten that.

When Cliff left, Alma and Boyd became permanently and very old, their correct age. When vigor or hope stirred in them, it was almost always perhaps because they found themselves talking of him.

The day Cliff had reported for induction into the army, he had thrown out all his clothes, except the few he wore to the induction center, and he had left these all in a pile, in the middle of his sleeping-room.

Weeks later, home on vacation, Alma had gathered up these clothes, soiled and mussed, holding them as carefully as if she wished not to lose all the folds and creases Cliff had left behind in them, and then putting them gently just as they were in an immense cedar chest in which no other garment was stored, and closing and locking the lid.

When the telegram had come announcing that he was missing, she had found herself almost unconsciously standing over the cedar box, but she had not opened it. She had never opened it to this day, because part of her mind, the part which delivered the speeches, said that Cliff was not dead and that one day, most unexpectedly, in the midst of trivial matters, he would walk in.

Alma had forgotten that if Cliff did walk in, he would no longer be a boy. He would be a mature man, a veteran.

But the cedar chest assuaged many a care which beset her. Sometimes in the late afternoon before she went down to make supper for Boyd, she would pass her hand ever so slightly over the chest, and a feeling of hope came to her, as inexplicable as it was profoundly moving.

Cliff had not been tidy, she might have written down in the record book, but her hand had not even moved in the

32

direction of the pen. He was accustomed to leave things in the middle of the floor, had no fixed place for any of his belongings, and therefore never remembered where anything was. Often he would put a soiled shirt or pair of shorts away in a bureau drawer and not think of them or find them for six weeks or half a year later. More often than not he lost his cufflinks and never found them again, so that in her absence, he or Boyd would be compelled to sew buttons on the impractical French cuffs. He had lost two wrist watches, and since he always lost gloves, he gave up wearing them.

Alma often wondered what had happened to him in the army, where he perforce must have had to be neat, orderly, prompt, and in line.

Perhaps Cliff had learned to be all these things in the army, Alma decided. Boyd had hinted as much, and then they had been informed he had been awarded the Purple Heart, a phrase that froze her with nausea.

And again, Alma caught herself thinking about her nephew in the present, in what she had once seen described somewhere as the "specious present." She felt often, confusing time, that Cliff was both at home with her and in the army. She expected him at one moment to come into the house and sit down to supper with her and Boyd, and the next moment, she was waiting to receive a letter from his APO address.

The clock in the east room chimed.

How odd, how terrifying, and yet how soothing, she thought, putting down the record book, that time runs out.

First we are here, she said to herself, being this sort of person and then so little later we have lost all track of that time and who we were then, until some trifle brings us back to that period for a brief lightning-illumined second, then back again to the now.

"Daily scandal sheet," Boyd greeted her with his customary early evening remark, putting down the *Sentinel* in Alma's lap.

Sometimes she responded to this hackneyed greeting in a feminine pleased way, again in a crabbed half-audible grunt.

Today, this late afternoon, half-dozing in her confused memories of time and the nephew, she merely moistened her lips, saying nothing.

"Everything all right?" Boyd asked faintly.

"I'll need some things from the store," she replied in her scolding voice.

Then she stopped to discover if she did need anything indeed.

"I'll go up the street for them in just a minute," he made use of her indecision.

"We need cooking oil, I am almost sure," she began to enumerate. "Some cheese to go with the pie, that is, if you'd like pie . . ."

He had gone to the door that led off the sitting room while she was making her list, opened it, and vanished.

From behind the door, she could hear him urinating.

Tonight she did not even resent the sound, which often made her irritable during the entire supper hour. The falling spray of his water suddenly meant nothing to her.

He came out with his right hand still touching his fly.

"Shall I write down the list of things?" She made her same daily query to him, and her hands clasped one another.

"I got it all in my head," he replied, and his hand touched his hat, which he had just put on.

"You might bring back some whipping cream," she said as a last-minute addition.

"Is that the works then?"

She nodded.

When he had finally gone, she suddenly remembered she had not heard him flush the toilet. Studying for a moment the tiny door leading off the sitting room, she walked slowly over to it, opened it, and went into the closet, looked down into the bowl, and flushed quickly.

She decided to wash her hands in the kitchen where there was a fresh cake of verbena soap.

She washed her hands slowly and deliberately like a surgeon, allowing a thick suds to reach as far as her wrists. Rinsing them, she dried them on a tiny face towel, embroidered with violets, which had belonged to her mother.

Often in the evening, they made a practise of turning out all the lights and sitting in the dark, talking. Those who passed by outside might have mistaken the absence of light to mean they were watching television. However, they had no set, neither Boyd nor Alma having the least desire to have to watch as well as to hear something which probably, in the end, could concern them very little.

Once they were seated in the dark, the emptiness and timelessness of the present receded a little. In this special prepared dark, their ages became ambiguous, and they might therefore have belonged again to any vigorous decade of their lives.

As they talked to one another in the dark, it even seemed to them that they were living their entire lives all at once, and were in command of their total personalities. Friends and relatives long dead entered into their conversation, and the hard implacable void of contemporaneity was dissipated. One could, so to speak, see land, breathe air. The night had lifted from night.

The sound of the blue jays' piercing cry always meant that morning was far advanced. In a half hour or so after the jays cried, one would hear the ketchup factory whistle announce noon and lunchtime.

Alma remembered how Cliff had sometimes come in from his work on the yard or some other household chore for a bite to eat, and the jays had called sharply each time he came into the house, closing the screen door behind him.

"Cliff, would you enjoy a dish of fresh strawberries?"

She could hear her own voice coming to her out of the recesses of the years.

Coming back to the present, she stood over the kitchen table, looking down at the recipe for Parker House rolls, for she had decided to present a baker's dozen of these as a surprise to Clara and Faye.

Her own mother had never had to refer to this particular recipe book, even though it was she who had copied down the instructions in the firm precise handwriting of that age; the recipes had been all—even down to the French ones—second-nature to *her*. Mother had written them down, as she explained to Alma one day, merely because others might want to consult them after she was gone.

THE PROFESSOR

4

SHORTLY after Alma had purchased the record book only to find that she could not put pen to its paper, a person went by her house who, she felt instinctively, might hold the key to her problem, and from whom a word or suggestion could unlock in herself all the things which she wished to write down about Cliff. This was Professor Mannheim.

In the days of Cliff, he had lived with his German-born wife in a wooden-frame house directly adjoining Alma's property on the west. After Cliff had gone into service, Professor Mannheim, following the onset of an attack of gout, became for a while badly crippled, and had as a consequence sold out to Alma so that he might move to closer proximity of his classes at the college. Alma had then torn down his house to allow her an unobstructed view, with a chance to see the sunset.

Alma stood at the kitchen window today watching the professor hobble past. He was extremely old in appearance now, partly owing to the fact the doctor insisted he walk with a cane. Near the college, he refused to employ one, for he was still vain about his personal appearance, but farther from home, he was seldom without it, though he still refused to wear his glasses in public, and it was his poor eyesight as much as his gout which caused him to stumble along like a much older man.

In the days of Cliff, Professor Mannheim had been a handsome vigorous man who belied his years with thick black indomitably curly hair, and an almost abnormally intense gaze—it was his hair and eyes perhaps which had made him a kind of idol of the co-eds in his history classes. The students in general ignored his political views, if they heard them at all—views at one time believed dangerous, if not treasonous—and concentrated on his magnetic physical presence, which was considerable, and which, while attracting the girls, was admired less than grudgingly by the boys.

Professor Mannheim stood out from the rest of the faculty of the college for Alma for another and only for another reason: he had declared to her unequivocally in the days when they were still neighbors that Cliff was his favorite, if not his most brilliant, student. This remark, while

36

it had pleased Alma in part, irked her too, for she felt somehow that there was greater understanding between Cliff and the professor than between Cliff and herself, or between Cliff and Boyd.

She therefore saw the professor hobble by today with mixed emotions, and she thought back suddenly for the first time in many years to the whispered scandals concerning Professor Mannheim, scandals now in a new decade nearly forgotten, and which Alma, in her persistent severance from the life of the town, had learned of only by accident, in the following way.

Professor Mannheim's first wife, Elsa, who was now dead, had also been very fond of Cliff. Isolated both from the faculty and the townspeople by reason of a natural shyness and also through her lack of command of English, Elsa— Alma had been certain—confided unwisely but fully to Cliff certain secrets of marriage and more specifically her suspicions of Professor Mannheim's indiscretions with co-eds.

Alma based this strong conjecture on her having surprised Cliff one summer afternoon holding a distressing conversation with Elsa, the latter weeping and crying within earshot, "You must never repeat what I have told you about the professor."

Cliff never did repeat what Elsa Mannheim had revealed.

Alma had learned of Professor Mannheim's "activities" later through, of all people, Mrs. Van Tassel who, having visited Maple Grove Cemetery late one afternoon (she had her own key to the cemetery gate) realized, when she had reached the road outside, that she had left her purse behind on the family plot. Fetching a flashlight from the sexton's house, she had insisted on returning alone to her family burial ground. What had been her surprise therefore when turning on her flashlight she had discovered Professor Mannheim lying with a young girl in an adjoining plot.

She had caught them, as she told Alma, in the absolute act.

Mrs. Van Tassel herself was certain that the guilty pair had not recognized her. Professor Mannheim himself had cried out like a stuck pig, and the girl had wept hysterically under his smothered embrace. Their physical involvement at the moment, however, had made it impossible for them to disentangle themselves, and there they had lain in the sudden illumination of her flashlight, helpless and miserable, while Mrs. Van Tassel picked up her purse and, having to halt every few paces in the grip of her own emotion, slowly made her way to the front gate of the cemetery.

As she reached the gate, and succeeded in closing the heavy iron door behind her, young Bill Pfeiffer, who was driving past in his florist delivery truck, caught sight of her. "I was never so glad to see anybody in my life," Mrs. Van Tassel used to cry in the days when she told this story of her experience. She had known the moment she saw Bill Pfeiffer that she would not have been able to get home unaided, and of course she forgot both the sexton and his flashlight.

How many years ago that was Alma could determine by watching the shuffling gait of Professor Mannheim as he finally disappeared from view. And the first Mrs. Mannheim was dead, and he had, quite expectedly, remarried, and his second wife, quite expectedly, was one of his former students.

But today the professor spent all his leisure time growing all known varieties of cactus, and seemed perfectly satisfied to spend his evenings in the company of his present wife.

Professor Mannheim had never been in Alma's house since the days of Cliff, and she knew, of course, that he would never be again.

At one time she had boasted that such a moral leper would never step into her front room. But today she felt neither satisfaction nor pride in such a sentiment. Professor Mannheim's moral obloquy did not reach her any longer. A new generation of students and faculty saw in him now only an elderly scholar waiting for retirement and pensioning, and to her he was only a person who brought back memories of Cliff, memories of herself, as she had been, at that time, somehow so much more important, so much more *doing*.

As a coincidence that morning, shortly after Professor Mannheim had gone past the kitchen window, Mrs. Van Tassel paid a call, crossing over from her back yard to Alma's, where the latter was now inspecting her myrtle bed.

"Professor Mannheim doesn't look very strong or well," Alma remarked from her crouching position over the myrtle bed, before she had even wished Mrs. Van Tassel good morning.

"*Who* doesn't?" Mrs. Van Tassel said in a hoarse loud voice.

"If he doesn't take care of himself, he won't be with us much longer, I fear." Alma pulled out a few dead leaves from the bed, and touched the new green ones softly. "Don't you think he looks bad?" Alma went on, looking up now at Mrs. Van Tassel, who still did not fully realize who was meant.

Rising, Alma said, "Come on inside and have a piece of

cake. I took it out of the oven only a couple of hours ago."

"Really, I should be going back," Mrs. Van Tassel said unemphatically.

"You could stand a bite," Alma told her.

The two women walked with bent heads into the kitchen. Alma brought out her chocolate cream cake which, in her mother's day, had won a prize at the county fair.

"Oh, that's far too generous, and at this time of day!" Mrs. Van Tassel said when Alma handed her a helping of the cake. "Goodness, what an aroma though!"

Mrs. Van Tassel bit into the cake.

Alma sat down beside her guest and began eating her portion of cake.

"You know," Alma began again, "when the first Mrs. Mannheim was alive, the professor ate so much more, and better. His second wife isn't much of a cook. They eat out a good deal."

As if reconciled to this subject of conversation, Mrs. Van Tassel said:

"The first Mrs. Mannheim was a perfect wife for any man. . . . Poor Elsa," she added, touching her mouth with a paper napkin.

Mrs. Van Tassel stopped after saying this. It was clear that she did not want to talk about Professor Mannheim, but it was also clear that Alma did, and that talking about Professor Mannheim was part of Alma's strategy in getting to another subject she wanted talked over even more.

"Everybody knows that Professor Mannheim has always drunk a good deal of alcohol," Alma said, though this aspect of the professor's character had never been much discussed in the town. "But with the first Mrs. Mannheim, he ate a great deal too, and his one bad habit was crossed out by his wife's table."

"If drinking had been just *all*," Mrs. Van Tassel surrendered to the weight of the past.

"Well, it has to be all just now," Alma said, a peculiar mixture of regret and judgment in her tone. "Considering his appearance, I mean, he can't very well do much."

Alma put her plate down.

"How *do* you do it?" Mrs. Van Tassel cried, gay now, pointing with her fork to the last morsel of the cake.

"Eat another piece," Alma said gravely.

"I'd pop," Mrs. Van Tassel told her.

"You're not on a diet," Alma urged her.

Mrs. Van Tassel refused with a girlish *No* and a laugh.

"You know, Cliff *liked* Professor Mannheim," Alma said swiftly.

"Oh." Mrs. Van Tassel was now grave.

"Professor Mannheim lent him so many books. He was a real influence on Cliff. Cliff spent hours there, you know."

"Well, it never affected Cliff, I'm sure." Mrs. Van Tassel rolled her eyes vaguely. "Cliff was such a . . . good boy."

"Of course we know Cliff didn't know about Professor Mannheim," Alma intoned, and then stopping, colored violently.

Mrs. Van Tassel had accepted her second piece of cake, and could only chew helplessly now, her eyes wandering about the room, a bit out of focus.

"Oh, but it's all so long ago," Alma said suddenly, and both Cliff and Professor Mannheim vanished like characters in a book whose covers one has snapped shut with impatience and finality.

"I never think of it, Alma," Mrs. Van Tassel .put her own empty plate down. "It all does seem a thousand years ago." She meant the cemetery and Professor Mannheim.

"You have closer-at-home troubles," Alma moved in.

Mrs. Van Tassel made a gesture to show that she was not willing to discuss Mrs. Hawke.

"You don't have to put up with her," Alma went on, coaxing.

"Things aren't quite that simple," Mrs. Van Tassel sighed, and gave in again to Alma's choice of topics.

"I think you can just tell her to go, Mrs. Van Tassel. That is, if you *want* her to go."

Alma folded her arms.

Mrs. Van Tassel considered the advice she had not come for.

Alma shifted in her chair in the silence that followed.

"You always make everything out to be so easy, Alma," Mrs. Van Tassel brought out with more vigor than usual. "Your mother used to remark on that."

"Oh, I'm aware of some of my failings," Alma laughed uneasily.

"I don't know whether you are or not," Mrs. Van Tassel remained firm and a little severe, almost unpleasant, so that one might not have known there had been cake and friendship here.

"You see, I owe Mrs. Hawke four thousand dollars," Mrs. Van Tassel said.

Alma went somewhat white, then blushed.

"I see you're surprised, and I guess disappointed," Mrs. Van Tassel commented, with a certain satisfaction in her manner.

"I'm hurt, perhaps," Alma admitted. "Why didn't you come to me?"

"Oh, I always thought of you as away, I guess . . . and

40

it was all so on the spur of the moment. I had to have the house repaired, you know. That was two years ago. It was something that had to be done or the whole property would have just gone to rack and ruin. And then Mrs. Hawke paid me a call."

Mrs. Van Tassel looked down at the small rag rug, her eyes suddenly as vacuous and distracted as those of Professor Mannheim's.

"Well, she didn't move in with you in exchange for the debt!" Alma cut through the chain of events leading to Mrs. Hawke's advent.

"No, no, I must say that for her," Mrs. Van Tassel shook her head. "She pays me her rent regular . . . And then she brings me so many things!"

Mrs. Van Tassel pushed back a brown hairpin which nearly came loose as she passed her hand over the back of her head.

"What, may I ask, does she bring you?" Alma inquired, coldly alert.

Mrs. Van Tassel fidgeted, her hand half-going up to the stray hairpin again. "Oh, delicacies . . . in the grocery line, you know."

"Ahem." Alma did not rein in her disapproval.

"It's been an awful struggle, you know, since Mr. Van Tassel passed on," the older woman made a gesture of surrender.

"*I* would have been glad to lend you the money," Alma said firmly, controlling carefully the scolding edge of her voice, but not wanting to hear again about the death of Mr. Van Tassel some twenty odd years ago.

"Thank you, Alma," Mrs. Van Tassel said brightly. "I have valued your friendship—well, more than you'll ever know. But this Mrs. Hawke affair—it was just fate, I guess."

"Owing her money doesn't mean she has to take over your house," Alma's voice came cold and decisive.

"I know that, Alma. But I feel I understand her a bit better than—some people. She lost a husband too, and now she has no one, you understand . . . We have come to have a lot in common. You see, it was her idea I try to get you to sell the plot of land between your house and the Bakers'. We would operate a small greenhouse, she thought, to keep us both busy."

Alma ignored the greenhouse. "Isn't an institution the place for Mrs. Hawke? With her money and all, she could go where she could get the best professional care, and be cured."

"She thinks she can lick the habit if she stays out of an institution," Mrs. Van Tassel said. "And she *is* trying."

"Oh, my *dear*. With that cane and all! *Trying?*"

"She is trying to lick the habit." Mrs. Van Tassel was unyielding about this one point. "And I want to help her."

"I'm afraid she's brought *you* down," Alma said, and anger had leaped into her voice.

"No, Alma." Mrs. Van Tassel's voice was comforting now and calm, more what it had been in the days when she had been Alma's mother's friend. "Don't you worry about me now, Alma."

"I do, and I mean to go on worrying. She's not right for your house!"

"But I owe her ..."

"Nothing!"

Alma had had her outburst, and she could be friendlier now, but it was clear from her manner that she had a plan.

"You talked so *forgiving* a while ago about old Professor Mannheim, who was, God knows, a leper." Mrs. Van Tassel sounded hurt and bewildered.

"Oh, he was foolish, of course." Alma dismissed the subject.

"Foolish?" Mrs. Van Tassel pretended she could not have heard aright.

"Those co-eds he took out were no better than he was." Alma invented this statement on the spot.

"Oh, Alma!" Mrs. Van Tassel showed extreme pain now. "You shouldn't even think such a thing."

"Mrs. Hawke doesn't mean just to destroy herself, you know," Alma went back doggedly to their first topic.

"Alma, Alma." Mrs. Van Tassel half-rose from her chair.

"Make her leave." Alma put her hand on Mrs. Van Tassel's shoulder. "I'll give you the four thousand—today, if you like. But don't go on with that woman and her cane. It brings the wrong note to the neighborhood!"

"My dear," Mrs. Van Tassel gasped.

"Think over what I'm saying," Alma rose now, and Mrs. Van Tassel stood up unsteadily to her full height.

"I have to think of her, too," the older woman urged this thought upon Alma again.

"You have to think of yourself ... You very good people are the first to fall!" she warned.

"I can't say anything to that."

"You don't need to. Go home and think over what I tell you. But you can't go on with her and be safe."

"What do you know about Professor Mannheim?" Alma asked Boyd a few days later as they sat gazing absently at different sections of the *Sentinel*, and from which Alma occasionally would snip with her shears a column for her files.

"What?" Boyd answered, meaning this time, not that he had not heard, but that he could not believe what he had heard.

"I said what do you know about Professor Mannheim. I don't see why that should surprise you so very much."

"God, I never think of him," Boyd replied, tightening one of his shoe laces.

"You must have known *about* him then—years ago," Alma said looking out the window in the general direction of Mrs. Van Tassel's.

"I don't live in the past as much as you do, Alma." He raised his deaf man's voice.

"You find your daily life pretty thrilling, I expect," she said.

He pretended deafness now.

"Professor Mannheim is a typical Dutchman," Boyd finally remarked.

"You mean he's German, don't you," she corrected him.

"I mean just what I said."

"Do you know if he saw a great deal of Cliff?" Alma asked in a loud clear voice.

There was a long high silence during which Boyd's jaw muscles worked vigorously. Alma studied his face closely, and then looked away. She knew he was very angry that she had asked this question.

"I don't think Cliff and he saw one another *at all*," Boyd finally exploded.

"Why then are you so mad I asked?" Alma did not back down.

"Are you warming over old town gossip?" he roared at her.

"No, I don't believe I am." Her firmness caught an edge of his anger.

"A man's private life is his own affair," Boyd observed with more calm.

"You would apply that to murder, too, I suppose," Alma commented.

"I would not."

"You could write Professor Mannheim, then, a blank check for moral rectitude," Alma bore down.

"Well, I couldn't write anybody a blank check for that, not even you."

Alma cleared her throat and rising walked to the corner of the living room where she grew her flowers. She touched a new leaf on her geraniums.

"All I wondered," she began again with a curious mixture of bashfulness and arrogance, "is whether Professor

Mannheim saw much of Cliff—saw enough to know about him—to be able to tell about him."

She clasped her hands together, and then catching herself in the gesture, like an amateur actor corrected by the director, she brought her arms down heavily to her sides.

"For God's sake," Boyd said, softening a bit, and looking away from her in embarrassment, "why can't you forget about Cliff for a while. *Let him rest in peace.*"

He winced at the sound of his own concluding statement, but Alma merely stood impassive and expressionless as on the days when her own hearing was especially poor.

Then as if to emphasize more particularly that she had not heard Boyd's last remark, she said in her special voice adjusted for his deafness:

"There were very serious scandals about Professor Mannheim some years ago, which reached the town as well as the campus."

Boyd made clicking sounds in his mouth of contempt and derision.

"Always digging up the past!" he said at last. "Never letting well-enough alone . . . That's the woman for you. Digging up what ought to have been forgotten long ago."

"You seem to be defending him on all counts," she cried, stung.

"Defending, poppycock. I don't know enough about him to defend him. But I do know that he behaves himself now, so far as I can see."

"All I wanted to know before you lost your temper," she went on, "is whether Professor Mannheim and Cliff saw a great deal of one another . . ."

"And I say let Cliff rest in peace!" He cut her off with something approaching brutality. "He's done his duty by his country!"

He threw the *Sentinel* to the floor, but then at the look of annihilation on his sister's face, he slowly gathered the sheets of the paper together again, and held them quietly in his lap.

"I'm sorry, Alma," he said, but she gave no evidence of having heard him.

"You see," she began, strolling up and down the living-room as she often did when alone, "I had planned, as you know, to write a little something about Cliff . . . and the thought that the professor had known him—as a student—naturally occurred to me . . ."

"Why shouldn't you see the professor, if that's the tree you're barking up?" Some of his old vexation came back under the sudden kindness he had just assumed.

"I just couldn't believe he would have known or under-

44

stood our Cliff!" She confronted him with this statement as if it contained her whole problem.

"What Professor Mannheim may have done in his private life—if he did anything," Boyd intoned, "and what he was in his classroom were two different things. I'm sure, for instance, he must have had a good influence on Cliff," Boyd soothed his sister with this fiction. "If he had any influence at all," he added under his breath.

She waited.

"And if you're going to write your memorial," and Boyd stopped on that word.

"Yes," she cried in her old imperious manner.

"Then there's no reason why you shouldn't go and see anybody you please about it," he brought out at last.

A QUESTION OF AFFILIATION

5

IN the midst of Alma's perplexities whether to visit Professor Mannheim and how to write the memorial to Cliff, Faye Laird unexpectedly dropped in for an early afternoon call. Perhaps to celebrate the end of classes for the semester, Faye had brought with her a huge assortment of early summer flowers.

As Alma put the flowers in water in some Japanese vases which had once gone begging in her gift shop, she asked Faye the routine questions about the end of the academic year.

"How is your mother's mind?" Alma asked in her sudden blunt way. "Is there any evidence of improvement, I mean," she added, seeing Faye's expression of open-mouthed distress.

Faye replied only after Alma had looked up twice from arranging the flowers. "I'm never without hope for Mother." Then after emitting what Boyd had once described as her "tuneless educated woman's laugh," Faye went on with a certain incisive edge to her voice:

"Clara Himbaugh came over two days ago to pray for Mother."

Alma had not quite arranged all the flowers in the vases, but on hearing this last remark, she made haste to crowd the remaining stems into water, and take her seat beside Faye in her own mother's rocking chair.

"I hardly think that's Clara's place," Alma took up the matter at once.

Faye considered this very briefly. "Clara said she knew God would cure Mother," and Alma immediately detected a peculiar note, rare for Faye, in the latter's voice.

"But you have your own church, child!" Alma brought out, though for the moment she found she had forgotten whether Faye was a Methodist or a Baptist, and she could not recall offhand the name of the minister of either of those churches in Rainbow.

"I had been through so terribly much with Mother just as the semester was ending . . . And then one day when I felt I could not endure it another moment—Clara appeared

46

as if out of nowhere," Faye explained. "So I let her go in and pray for Mother," she told Alma.

"I don't think Reverend Alter would care for your letting such a thing happen at all." Alma had remembered in a flash that Faye was a Methodist.

"God is God," Faye replied more firmly, but her apologetic tone was still predominant.

"I hope *you* are not the one who is going to turn Scientist," Alma cried.

Faye stared at the summer flowers she had brought, rigid and wooden in the Japanese vases.

"It's been my worst year, Alma. Mother is getting to be nearly bedridden."

"But you haven't yet in all this time called in a specialist," Alma said, and a harsh almost angry note was in her voice.

"But Dr. Haynes said it was beyond any doctor. That's why, I guess, I haven't considered a specialist."

Faye loosened a ring on her finger which Alma thought had always resembled—to the point of being embarrassing —an engagement ring.

"Don't for pity's sake turn to Science!" Alma warned, looking away from her guest. "Remember what happened to Clara Himbaugh herself when she let Dr. Koontz pull her teeth without so much as an aspirin. And don't forget—"

"Just the fact Clara prayed for Mother helped *me* no end," Faye said. "Reverend Alter has never done a thing like that for us."

"That's his fault, not your church's," Alma proceeded.

"I can't help it, Alma," Faye said sweetly but without yielding. She worked at her ring again, "I'm going to let Clara keep on coming."

"I see," Alma said, picking up her sewing basket and looking about in it. "I wanted to show you that exciting spool of thread that just came to the shop from Japan," she explained perfunctorily. "But I don't seem to be able to find it."

"It was nothing that Cliff sent you by chance?" Faye brought out with peculiar innocence.

Alma's cheeks went white, then a muddy red.

"This was a recent gift. A former teacher friend of mine," Alma said with unusual dryness even for her.

"You haven't been to church, that is your church, for quite a long time, have you, Alma," Faye observed in an absent-minded casual manner.

"I go on the important days," Alma replied. *"Always."*

"It would have helped you a lot, I mean, when you were so burdened awhile back about Cliff," Faye went on and

Alma knew by the way her voice shook how much effort this had taken. Nobody liked to mention Cliff in Alma's presence, unless permission for it had been granted by Alma and the nature of the discussion approved in advance by her.

"Prayer might even bring him home," Faye said, the last breath of courage in her voice.

"Faye," Alma cried, struggling to keep possession of herself. She rocked a bit, and pushed aside her sewing basket. "It would do no harm," Alma went on with her first subject, "if you called in a specialist from Cincinnati, say, or even New York. He could have a good look at your mother."

"Alma, I've been over all this with other doctors, and we had a specialist, for heaven's sakes, years ago. You've forgotten is all."

"One specialist is not enough," Alma warned, but there was little conviction now in her tone.

"You've never heard Clara Himbaugh pray, have you?" Faye said almost compulsively.

"Yes, unfortunately, I have. And I wish if she had to pray she could afford a good set of teeth."

"Alma, that remark is not worthy of you."

"There's no need in performing publicly if one's teeth whir like hers. Anymore than a cripple should appear in the ballet. Not everybody can pray, at least in public ..."

"Alma, we seem to be quarrelling," Faye whispered.

"I wanted to ask you, by the way," Alma brightened determinedly, rocking a bit in her chair, as if their spat over Clara and Science was many weeks past, "do you see much of Professor Mannheim when you're at the college?"

Alma's habit of abrupt change of subject—even nonsequiturs—was familiar to all her acquaintances, but the surprising mention of Professor Mannheim seemed almost sinister to Faye.

Alma, however, did not wait for an answer to her own question, which she herself evidently regarded as rhetorical.

"You see, Faye, I have been writing down a kind of biographical sketch of Cliff—until he gets home. It was an idea that just came to me," she explained, but as she said this she changed color, and stopped rocking.

"Did you know about it?" Alma spoke severely when she saw the peculiar look on Faye's features.

Faye shook her head.

"I must say you looked as though you did." Alma remembered how with uneasiness that the whole idea of the memorial had stemmed from Clara Himbaugh.

"I wondered why you asked about Professor Mannheim, I guess," Faye said with some puzzlement at Alma's discomfort, but she was tired, and as she spoke she rose from her chair.

A bit hurt that Faye had gotten up, Alma did not reply immediately, and then slowly rose from the rocking chair.

"I suppose you're thinking of the professor's old reputation," Alma said.

Faye merely looked blank.

"Don't tell me you've forgotten what he was." Alma attempted to speak in a jocular manner, but instead she sounded fanatic and menacing. "I wondered—is all— whether Professor Mannheim couldn't help me fill in the academic part of Cliff's career," Alma went on at last in the midst of Faye's continuing silence.

"I should think he might," Faye replied as close to indifference as she could bring her voice.

"Evidently you disapprove of my seeing him, or something!" Alma said stonily.

"Not in the least! Actually, I had forgotten his old scandal," Faye mused. She brushed a strand of hair from her forehead. "Time does fly, there's no getting around that." She laughed.

"Well, he never influenced Cliff in a moral sense, I'm sure," Alma said vaguely, observing her friend's impatience to be gone. "Faye, please sit down again," Alma suddenly implored her, "and I'll make us some hot chocolate. You could stand with a cup."

"I would love to," Faye replied, with a rush of warmth and understanding. "But I have to get home. Mother will be fidgeting something awful by now. You know she can only be without me for the shortest periods."

"Of course I understand," Alma replied. "But if you'll just step into the library here," she pointed to the west room. "I have something to show you."

Faye half-entered the library, and Alma hurried to her desk and came back with the book of records.

"I'm writing down everything I can remember about him, you see," Alma extended the book to her friend. But having opened the blank sheets of the record book, she stopped. There were heavy tears in Faye's eyes; at the moment Alma extended the book to her, they fell ostentatiously to her cheeks and lips.

Alma, dry-eyed, looked away.

"I think Professor Mannheim would have lots of ideas for you," Alma heard Faye's bright voice, which in the silence of the room might almost have been mistaken for Clara Himbaugh's.

"I mean to go see him as soon as possible," Alma said, and she came forward to relieve Faye of the record book.

They kissed briefly at the door.

"Regards to your mother," Alma said in a voice nearly unrecognizable as hers.

That evening after supper, as Boyd leafed through an old issue of the *National Geographic*, Alma said: "I'm afraid we're in for an interesting little case of proselytizing right in the neighborhood."

"Who's converting who?" Boyd spoke with abrupt ill-temper, and he plumped the magazine down on his knee.

"Clara Himbaugh is bringing Faye Laird over to Christian Science," she shouted to him.

Boyd whistled.

"There's no doubt about it." Alma warmed up to his obvious show of interest: "On pretense of praying for old Mother Laird, Clara has been beating a path to their house for the past week or so. And if you ask me, I think Faye is ripe for going over to Clara's faith. She feels her youth is gone and her chances for marriage nil, and I suppose she's clutching at a straw."

"I should think that with her going to college all her life, Faye would know better than to take up with Christian Science," Boyd shook his head.

"Oh, educated people are no more immune from making fools of themselves than others. As I told Faye, she has her own church, why doesn't she turn to it in perplexity."

"By George, Clara Himbaugh would have had a tough time of it converting Mother Laird when *that* old girl had her marbles," Boyd reflected. "If Faye has any of her mother's spunk, she'll not let Clara get to first-base."

"That's just what Faye lacks, spunk," Alma scolded. "She was *weeping* in here today."

"What the devil about?"

"I don't know what it was," Alma was evasive. "I expect her mother and all. And never having got married..."

"Nobody can deny old Mother Laird ruined her life," Boyd said. "She was really in love with Bob Phillips that time."

"Faye seemed to think I should see Professor Mannheim about the memorial." Alma had shifted subjects, but cautiously and less emphatically than was customary for her.

"See him about what?" Boyd looked blank.

"About the biography I am writing on Cliff, of course!" Boyd looked down at the cover of the *National Geographic*.

"You remember what I told you about the memorial," she refreshed his mind.

"Yes, of course," he said impatiently. "And I told you

50

at that time if you wanted to see Professor Mannheim to see him."

"I gathered, though, that you didn't approve of it just the same."

"Approve hell. I told you to do as you please since that's what you always do anyhow. But since you ask me again, I'll tell you. I think letting a third party go to the professor would be in better form."

"A third party?" Alma was incredulous.

"That's right. For one thing I think Professor Mannheim is still sore over the price you gave him when you bought his house."

"Oh, fiddle. This is the first time I ever heard of it," she scoffed, but her face colored.

"Well, he thinks you soaked him," Boyd was emphatic.

"Why, I asked him again and again if he felt my offer was fair. He always said *yes* with his absurd German hiss."

"All I know is he has complained a good many times to both college and town people that you *took* him."

Alma rocked in her chair. "A fine time to complain after all these years . . . But I don't quite know what you mean, just the same, about a third party." Her voice was querulous.

"There's only one person in this neck of the woods who could really go to Professor Mannheim and come back with any information out of him," Boyd said.

Alma's mouth opened gently.

"Can't you guess who I mean?" Boyd taunted.

"No, I can't," she said, and her irritation was matched only by her curiosity.

"Mrs. Barrington, of course!" he pronounced with his kind of triumph.

Alma's silence bespoke agreement, however reluctant. Then she remembered: "But she's in Washington, D.C."

"Mrs. Barrington returned to Rainbow Center last night," Boyd informed her. "She can't take the summer in the capital, you know."

"The old monarch! Good grief," Alma cried.

Mrs. Barrington was, of course, the person one eventually had to see in Rainbow Center about anything of real importance. If Boyd and Alma had not mentioned her recently in their daily talk, it was, if anything, because her presence was felt too much.

Alma glanced out through the south window where, ensconced in grounds almost large enough for a forest preserve replete with every variety of tree, shrub, flower, vine and fence, one saw Mrs. Barrington's Victorian mansion rise stories above Alma's or any other house in Rainbow Center. Yet by its very vastness and grandeur, Mrs. Barrington's estate on Peninsula Drive marked the boundary and terminus of the town, rather than forming any real part of them. The significant thing about Mrs. B., as she was often called, was her arrivals and departures and not her sojourns. She was the *transient* spirit of Rainbow Center.

"Of course, Mrs. Barrington was once the chairman of the board of trustees of the college." Alma was making a careful evaluation of Boyd's advice.

"Oh, she's been everything," said Boyd, dismissing her reputation as a businss woman. "After all she must be a hundred!"

"Well, she'll never see eighty-five again," Alma was positive.

"Ninety at least," Boyd said. "She was nearly Mother's age."

"I suppose I should have just gone to Professor Mannheim in the first place without a peep to anybody," Alma complained.

"You can still see him if you want to, for God's sakes," Boyd told her. "I only thought—"

"I know. You only thought I would put my foot in my mouth."

"I think Professor Mannheim would tell Mrs. Barrington anything he knew at all about Cliff. He might even have his old compositions and exams. He keeps everything from his students, they say."

Boyd shifted under Alma's icy silence, but finally it was she who spoke.

"I suppose," she said, "if Mrs. Barrington asked anybody —especially a professor—to tell anything, it would be a royal command, and he'd have to tell her whether he knew anything or not. While if I asked the professor—"

"It was a question of delicacy is all," Boyd defended himself. "Professor Mannheim does not feel kindly toward us . . ."

"To me, you mean," Alma insisted.

"All right, to you."

"I soaked him."

"Well, as a matter of fact, I think you did," Boyd announced with quiet decision.

There was only the accelerated rocking of Alma's chair in reply. She was already thinking of her coming visit to Mrs. Barrington.

"ONE MUST DISCUSS SOMEBODY"

6

AFTER the letters from Cliff had stopped, Alma found it more and more difficult to remember the definite order of events. Things seemed to be happening without sequence, and all at once. There was no longer an orderly progression: Korea, hydrogen bombs, the conquest of outer space —all suddenly came to mean to her merely an interruption or postponement of regular and coherent daily events which could no longer be remembered conveniently.

The people who perhaps interested her most—Willard Baker, Mrs. Barrington, Professor Mannheim, Minnie Clyde Hawke, seldom or never appeared in her home. And those who did pay calls devoted large sections of their conversation to these very persons. And if Cliff occupied a major portion of her and Boyd's exchange, other absent (if not dead) persons took up the rest of her talk.

"One must discuss somebody!" Alma had exclaimed one day to Faye Laird in a sudden burst of gay self-derision.

She could hardly deny that all kinds of things were going on about her. Life did not stop. Not even, as she never tired of saying, in Rainbow Center. And the echoes of old scandals refused to die down.

Almost in the same manner in which Mrs. Van Tassel had been evasive with Alma about both Minnie Clyde Hawke and Professor Mannheim, and Faye had been evasive about Clara Himbaugh's visits to her mother, everybody in the town was evasive to her about Cliff.

In the deepening twilight of her life, she came more and more to the slow, conscious and terribly clear feeling that *they* all knew a great deal more about Cliff—not to mention what they knew about things in general, about *life*—than she could ever know. She, who had cared for him more than anybody else; she, to whom Cliff meant not just everything now but perhaps all there had ever been—she alone, still waited for his letters. Everybody else accepted Cliff as if he were permanently missing. Yet all these people who no longer expected him knew *more* about him than she could ever know. Even Boyd, she felt, knew more about Cliff than she did, and like the others he would be the first to deny it.

Now a new fear arose to assail Alma. The days of Cliff were so long ago that Professor Mannheim in his debilitated state might no longer remember exactly who Cliff was. Of course he would *remember* him—after all they had been neighbors, and Cliff was not just any student—but would the professor remember the right things, the things which Alma so wanted to know? Of course she would have been as hard put to tell what the *right things* were as she was to fill out the blank pages of the record book with the facts of Cliff's biography. And finally Professor Mannheim, like Boyd, was only a man and could never tell her—could never tell Mrs. Barrington, that is—the certain things she felt she must know if she were to write the memorial.

Cliff's biography—if he had one—was likely to consist of the very elements which a man would not be apt to tell a woman. Even supposing that the professor knew the elements, he might not be able to know or recognize the important ones—the real ones—in Cliff's life, and would perhaps content himself with relating anecdotes that could have happened to anybody.

As Alma was immersed in these cogitations, Boyd came into the front room with a package containing a pint of home-made sherbet which he had got as a gift from Emma Hotchkiss, principal caterer to the well-to-do in Rainbow Center and a woman who, in her younger days, had set her cap for Boyd. Alma had always grudgingly admitted (she could never approve of Emma's four marriages) that the caterer did make marvelous confections and ices.

As she took the package from Boyd, she said with effusive affability: "How *was* dear Emma?"

"What's the sudden good will toward Emma?" Boyd could not prevent a slight edge to his voice.

Alma controlled her own slight feeling of irritation. She knew, for one thing, that she must talk with Boyd again, and at length, over her proposed visit to Mrs. Barrington and over Mrs. Barrington's own *proposed* visit to Professor Mannheim, and it would not do now to spat over Emma Hotchkiss.

"I admire Emma's ability as a cook, and I have never begrudged her her local reputation," Alma shouted from the kitchen, dishing out the peach ice. She licked her fingers surreptitiously and was again amazed at what a great triumph the sherbet was. She could hardly refrain at that moment from a complete encomium.

"It's perfectly delicious," she said in a flat voice, bringing in a serving to Boyd. He noted she had got out her best chinaware, and she handed him a linen, not a paper, napkin. The spoon was silver, too.

"Glad something pleases you," he mumbled.

"Did I give you a generous enough serving?" she said, a bit of an edge now in her voice, for she did not want to alarm him with too kind or saccharine a manner as a beginning for her real talk with him.

Boyd shook his head a bit mournfully, perhaps anticipating something unpleasant which she now meant to bring up.

But Alma displayed no ill-temper, no hint of a tendency to be unkind today. "The old girl has not lost her touch," Alma began on her own serving of peach sherbet.

Boyd nodded, silent, giving his main attention to the pleasure of the sherbet. Then looking at her carefully and in the coaching voice he employed with his clients:

"Her mother, of course, was the *great* cook. When I used to visit the family, they always invited me to a bite of something. You should have tasted her Parker House rolls."

"I remember them," Alma said, but too low for his deafness.

"Her bread won prize after prize in State fairs all over the country. Won a national prize in Chicago."

Alma was not listening now. She was going over in her own mind the speech she had half-planned for Mrs. Barrington, and in a minute she wanted Boyd to hear her thinking out loud what she had planned for the old monarch. Even if his deafness did not take in quite all she said, saying the speech out loud would help her get up courage to go to Mrs. Barrington.

When she saw that he had finished his sherbet, she went to take the dish from him, saw a spot on his fresh shirt, daubed at it quickly with her pocket handkerchief, and then relieved him of the dish.

"What's the red-carpet treatment for?" he wondered as she walked out toward the kitchen.

Alma smiled, but did not reply immediately.

Boyd was soon buried again in the *Sentinel*.

Returning to the living room, Alma rocked for a few minutes, wondering how she could prepare him for her practice-speech for Mrs. Barrington. Even her praise of Emma's sherbet and her implied praise of Emma herself could not prepare him, she knew. Even kindness, outright kindness carried on for the space of a year, for years, would not prepare him for what she had to say.

"Do you suppose Mrs. Barrington really will see the professor for me?" She heard her own words loud and clear, if rather shaky in the upper register.

"Why wouldn't she see him for you?" Boyd said, lowering the paper briefly. "She'd be glad to, if you ask me." He put the paper up again quickly without waiting for Alma to reply.

"Perhaps if *you* broached the subject of my writing Cliff's biography," she made the suggestion in her faintest voice.

"*Me* ask her?" Boyd had heard her, and he looked out boldly from the *Sentinel*.

"I see you chat quite a bit with Mrs. Barrington as you go by her house," she said.

"News to me that I do," he said in his most self-possessed and severe manner.

"All right, you don't even know her then!" Alma cried. "After all, it was you who had the idea of a *third party*."

Boyd considered this. "I've seen from the beginning you were determined to write a biography or a memorial, or whatever term you wish to use, on the subject of Cliff. And Mrs. Barrington is certainly somebody who can give you a suggestion or two, beyond her getting anything out of old Mannheim. After all in her youth—though that was a devil of a while ago—she wrote stories for magazines."

"Well, I'm hardly writing a story," Alma's temper flared for a second. Then she added, penitently, "But I had forgotten about her being a writer, and I'm glad you reminded me."

"And she's a college graduate," Boyd could not resist this dig. "You've got a lot more in common with her than I have. See her, for God's sake. There's one thing about Mrs. B., too. She's not afraid of anybody or anything. She'd probably *grill* Mannheim if you asked her to."

"I expect you're right," Alma mused, and the thought did not seem an unwelcome one.

"But don't go expecting too much now," he shouted, and he rose as he spoke.

"And what in heaven's name do you mean by that?" She spoke with a kind of tolerant condescension, but there was now a note of alarm in her voice.

"Just what I say. Don't think that either an old woman of 90 or a professor crowding retirement is going to tell you enough about a young fellow of 18 or 19 to fill up a book with."

"I have enough to fill my book now with, if I want to," she shot back, and she got to her feet also. "But I want to know . . . well, the *formal* facts about him. What other people saw and knew about him. His academic record and so on. We both know all there is fundamentally to know about Cliff," she appealed to him.

The look of denial on Boyd's face, however, stopped her.

"We know Cliff, that's all," she said inaudibly.

"If you'll excuse me now," Boyd said, leaving the room.

Alma had completely forgotten to give him the speech she had rehearsed for Mrs. Barrington.

That night Alma lay in bed helpless with insomnia. Yet, as frequently happens with insomniacs, she dozed and dreamed from time to time. She heard Boyd get up at his usual time (he got dry about three A.M. without fail), take the tumbler down, rinse it, fill it, and take a long and gurgling drink. Then the toilet flushed. She was again prey to her wakefulness.

In her half-sleep, Alma had a long imagined interview with Mrs. Barrington in which a rather heated argument between the two women occurred, and although Mrs. Barrington under these circumstances may have lost the argument, Alma felt herself grow red with anger even in the privacy of her own bed.

Mrs. Barrington's fame in Rainbow Center rested not only on her mansion and wealth but on an affliction: in her youth she had lost her left foot in an accident so gruesome nobody had ever repeated the exact details, and she had worn an artificial limb ever since. The accident, so the story went, had changed Mrs. Barrington from a spoiled young newlywed into a resourceful and energetic woman of weight and responsibility in the community.

In addition to her property and her artificial foot, Mrs. Barrington enjoyed each summer an additional notoriety: the trumpet vine which grew over the north end of her two-acre estate. Once in bloom, the trumpet vine became, year after year, the inevitable topic of comment. Visitors from other counties half across the state came to view it. The vine itself covered in extent half a city block. During its flowering, Mrs. Barrington often appeared outdoors, limping and busy, assisted by a small crowd of college boys, directing as was her custom all the yard-work on her property, and bowing occasionally to some of the more appreciative "tourists."

Of course the trumpet vine was lovely, as Alma was the first to point out. But Mrs. Barrington made so much of it all. *Her* yard, *her* trumpet vine, Alma often complained of her to Boyd and to Faye Laird, *her* long supervision of the town and county and indeed the state. Mrs. Barrington never bothered to look at anybody else's yard or flowers. Oh no, she was too busy with her own.

Mr. Barrington—it now seemed implausible that there had been such a person—had been dead for more than a quarter of a century, but those, like Alma, who could remember that far back, recalled that he had played such an inconspicuous part in her life, had been seen so seldom with her in public (they even took their meals separately at home) that his actual death came like a mere corroboration to the public of the old suspicion that he had never existed at all.

Mr. B.'s passing, of course, made no change in the routine of the old monarch's life. The day after his funeral, which was expensive, if not showy, and as short in duration as local convention permitted, she was up and about as usual, commanding the gardener to transplant a bush and dig up an old rock garden which apparently no longer represented her taste, while other workmen were engaged in bringing from a favorite greenhouse some twenty miles away new sod for the west greensward.

Occupied as she was, however, Mrs. Barrington did give a glance now and then at Alma. She felt, it was clear, that if Alma was not precisely her equal—and who was?— she was at all events a "figure" even though only a grade-school teacher, and without a doubt something of a competitor. Alma could not, in other words, be ignored.

On the other hand, Mrs. Barrington pretty much refused to recognize her other neighbors. In the case of Faye Laird, she found the very thought of woman professor somewhat uncomfortable, and Mrs. Laird, of course, she already counted among the departed; she almost pretended not to remember who Clara Himbaugh was. She had never had to recognize Professor Mannheim socially, despite her former position as chairman of the board of trustees of the college. She spoke to Mrs. Van Tassel when this seemed unavoidable. Minnie Clyde Hawke she had not recognized in public since the latter had moved out of her own house and part of town to board with Mrs. V. T.

Surprisingly enough, Mrs. B. was often seen chatting— however briefly—with Willard Baker. He made her laugh, she said, but then there had been, after all, his distinguished family.

In her imagined talk Alma saw Mrs. B.'s mask of good breeding and civility drop. She said outright what Alma had always known the old monarch felt, namely, that her "things," her trumpet vine, her mansion and acres of property, were not simply the best in this state, but quite without doubt the best of their kind *anywhere*.

"I don't think you could possibly find a more beautiful vine anywhere," Alma heard Mrs. Barrington's damaged contralto. "Certainly none within motoring distance. For luxuriance, growth, beauty, size—there is nothing to compare with it, my dear." And Mrs. Barrington stretched upward to touch one of the highest stalks of the flowers.

"Mrs. Barrington, dear heart," Alma could hear her own voice now, "you and I have been neighbors for a good many years."

"Fifty odd," Mrs. Barrington's answer came from behind a stalk of blossoms.

Alma smiled, both in her imagined interview with Mrs. B. and actually beneath the covers of her bed.

"Yet during these fifty odd years," Alma said, "I have never yet heard you initiate any conversation or terminate one which did not have as its sole subject the pre-eminence of your own things."

She had purposely made her statement vague, and Mrs. Barrington seized on its vagueness at once.

"My own things, Alma?"

"Your possessions, your land, your this-and-that. Your *rule* here, let us say." Alma could hear her own mounting anger.

"It may be, dear, that my things, as you call them, are all that you remember from our talks together," Mrs. Barrington said, though not so tartly as she might have, and yet Alma was struck by the old girl's readiness at rejoinder, her calm and persistent invincibility.

"That may well be," Alma admitted, "but, no, I don't think it quite covers the psychology of the case. I remember only your things because it is simply all you talk about, you see. You have no other subject."

"But supposing this to be true, dear Alma—that I am bereft of any other subject but what you specify. Is this then such a crime in a very old woman?"

"I should say it was a serious fault, Mrs. Barrington, age aside."

"I see," Mrs. Barrington considered Alma's attitude. "Well, we have quarrelled," she brought out after an impressive pause, and her hand let go of a stalk of the trumpet vine which she had taken hold of during Alma's explosion.

Then quite unexpectedly as it might have done in real life, this imaginary conversation shot beyond the fore-knowledge of the imaginer.

"And Cliff, I suppose, is not one of your own things, as you put it," Mrs. Barrington's cold face came from behind the vine.

"You dare mention him in this connection." Alma's voice was lower than her usual pitch for Boyd's accustomed level of hearing, but clear enough for Mrs. B.'s.

"Very well, my dear. You began the argument—allow me to continue it. Cliff was as much to you in the way of one of *your* possessions, Alma, as my yard or my garden, my house or my trumpet vine, and while I have had the luxury of being able to talk about a good many of the *things*, I am afraid you had rather limited yourself to just the one subject. And now, my dear, I have a thousand things to do. Good day."

Mrs. Barrington abruptly left her, turning down a short side-path which led from the luxuriant trumpet vine to the small handsome tool-shed in the rear of the estate.

"Mrs. Barrington!" Alma called out.

Mrs. Barrington stopped on the garden path.

"I think I do owe you an apology," Alma went up to her. "We have been friends too long to talk like this. Too very long."

"I'm afraid you are much too used to saying to Boyd whatever pops into your head to remember that other people may not be quite so used to your outspokenness." Mrs. Barrington flashed a frigid but not altogether unpleasant smile at Alma. "Frankness is one thing in one's own home, quite another away from that home."

"I quite agree," Alma could hear her own weak apology.

"I'm afraid agreement, sweetheart, isn't quite enough this time. You've said very cruel things, you see. You've hurt people again and again. You go on hurting people."

"You shouldn't have mentioned Cliff!" Alma had gone quite off again in the same direction.

Mrs. Barrington stopped on this statement. She brought the long folds of her skirt over her artificial foot. Her teeth clicked a bit in the morning air.

"You wanted to mention him, Alma, and you ought to mention him more, if anything. I don't know whether he is dead or not, of course, but I have never been of those who have their minds made up, though I know you class me with those who have."

"I never said that," Alma protested, warning.

"You never had to, you looked it!" Mrs. Barrington was firm. "You looked it, and your looks told enough."

"I can't consider Cliff on the level with a trumpet vine."

"You don't need to," Mrs. Barrington told her. "But a lot of people think it's queerer for you to go on thinking about a missing nephew than it is for me to care all the time for my own back yard. Of the two of us peculiar old people, it's you they hold the odder," Mrs. Barrington brought out. "At least I can see what I'm doing."

"Well, you've held nothing back, Mrs. B.," Alma spoke in a whisper.

"I don't see how I could very well hold anything back since you nearly knocked it out of me in any case," Mrs. Barrington laughed. "But I think we should be friends. I don't see why we should fight."

Alma said nothing.

"Mind you, I don't think you're queer a bit, and I don't think there is any certainty Cliff is dead," Mrs. Barrington continued. "I've always had a feeling he was alive."

"Thank you," Alma said.

Mrs. Barrington's own subsequent silence underlined the irony of Alma's *thank you*, and the question of Cliff was dropped.

"Come have a cup of something with me," Mrs. Barrington ushered Alma toward her house, and there was nothing for Alma to do but follow her. And at that point Alma's imagined interview was over.

7

Two days later, while Alma was still screwing up her courage to make a real visit to Mrs. Barrington, she heard familiar voices coming from the old monarch's yard, and hastily glanced out from the south library window.

She was surprised and disgusted to see Boyd, hat in hand, going up the front walk to Mrs. Barrington, while the latter opened the door to him. Her brother entered the house somewhat sheepishly, it was clear, but *willingly,* she was certain. But she could not be certain whether Boyd had purposely gone there or whether Mrs. B. had merely called to him to come in, as she did from time to time.

"He'll botch everything!" She heard her own voice rise in the stillness of the library, and wheeling about her eye fell on the record book. Angry and confused, she picked the book up roughly and then put it down with a kind of combined fury and loving kindness which immediately brought to her mind Reverend Lindsay's somewhat frightening gesture of closing the Scriptures at the First Presbyterian Church, on high occasions.

She left the library and came into the living room where she walked up and down heavily.

The idea struck her to invite Fay Laird over for lunch. She must see somebody, she must talk to somebody, however indirectly, about Boyd's being with Mrs. B., about Mrs. B. in relation to Professor Mannheim, and about the whole problem of her writing the memorial.

Faye's twangy fatigued voice answered the telephone.

"Don't say you can't now, for pity's sake," Alma forestalled a refusal. "I've got to see somebody."

"As a matter of fact," Faye assumed her formal classroom voice over the phone, "Clare Himbaugh is here with Mother, and I could come over."

"Then please do so," Alma said peremptorily, and hung up.

As Faye came through the back door into the kitchen, Alma kissed her, saying: "I thought you would never get here."

Out of breath, Faye sat down in the comfortable garden chair Alma had brought in especially for her from the summer house.

"Drink this while you're getting your energy back." Alma handed her a glass of fruit juice.

"No juice, if you please," Faye said. "I've drunk so much orangeade today I have a sour stomach."

"Some coffee then." Alma took the glass of juice away. Faye nodded.

"Well, your mother's safe with Clara, at any rate," Alma began. She turned up the gas jet under the coffee pot.

"They're watching the circus on TV," Faye volunteered.

"Good," Alma said, and she poured the heated coffee into a blue cup and gave it to Faye. "Meantime, I've gotten myself into the worst mess." Alma sat down with her own cup of coffee. She stirred vigorously in the bottom of the cup, although she did not take sugar or cream.

Relieved at least that Alma had passed on from Clara Himbaugh and her mother to something else, Faye perked up a bit and even listened with more attention than usual.

"I've got stalled as you know in writing Cliff's memorial," Alma began in the same matter-of-fact tone she might have used years before in discussing her master's thesis at Teachers' College. "Then I made up my mind, as I told you, to see Professor Mannheim. Just as I was about to go to him, Boyd put his foot down."

Faye dropped her cup heavily to her saucer, perhaps in incredulity at the vision of Boyd Mason putting his foot down.

"Boyd, you see, feels it's Mrs. Barrington who should see Professor Mannheim, if anybody's to see him, about getting information regarding Cliff—especially his academic career."

Faye's features were expressionless except for her mouth which sagged unaccountably.

"I can see you don't share Boyd's opinion," Alma remarked, but she conveyed neither relief nor satisfaction in her tone.

"The whole thing more or less confuses me, Alma," Fay cried, lighting a Camel.

"What 'thing' are you talking about," Alma inquired, unable not to give a critical glance at the cigarette.

"Well, your *memorial* of Cliff," Faye removed a tobacco particle from her tongue.

"But why on earth should that confuse anybody?" Alma asked with condescending frigidity.

"Oh, the purpose I understand perfectly," Faye rallied with warmth. "But the choice of material—I mean what do you intend to put down?"

Alma flushed, rose, took the coffee pot from the gas and poured two fresh cups, though Faye had scarcely touched hers.

"My problem isn't an easy one, of course. Especially now that the old monarch is in on it."

"How do you know that?" Faye wondered.

"Boyd is over there this very minute at Mrs. Barrington's and he'll spill the beans. He always tells her everything. They gossip together like fools. And of course she'll go to Professor Mannheim."

"Why, they're enemies," Faye said, meaning the professor and Mrs. B.

"Since when?" Alma scoffed.

"Since the beginning. It was Mrs. Barrington, you know, who nearly got Professor Mannheim dismissed when she was chairman of the board of trustees. He wrote all those articles on Marx, you know, and then when the moral turpitude charges came up, even though nobody could prove them, she felt he should be let out."

"Oh, that was ages ago, dearest."

"Ages ago to us, maybe," Faye quibbled. "But I doubt if Professor Mannheim has forgotten it or that he doesn't lie awake at night sometimes worrying about it, and about Mrs. B."

"You see, according to Boyd," and Alma paused as if considering for the last time the value of any of her brother's evidence, "according to him, I could never go to Professor Mannheim because of his ill-feelings toward me. And now you tell me he has, if anything, still greater feelings of resentment toward Mrs. B.!"

"I don't think Professor Mannheim has very kindly feelings toward any of us," Faye said somewhat warmly again. "And I can't blame him."

"Oh, Faye, whatever do you mean by that?"

"I mean nobody in Rainbow Center has treated him as he deserves to be treated, as a scholar deserves to be treated. Certainly the college never had the decency to promote him, despite his achievements."

"I was never aware that I had mistreated him until Boyd told me the other day he thinks I never reimbursed him properly for his house and property."

"We've all looked down on him," Faye said.

Alma sipped her coffee.

"Well, as usual, I've done the wrong thing," Alma remarked a moment later.

"Don't blame yourself," Faye smoked greedily now, having set her coffee cup down. "There's no point in our feeling guilty *all* the time for what we've made of ourselves."

Alma looked up indignantly. "I don't feel guilty about anything, I'm afraid."

64

"Of course you don't. And if Boyd has told Mrs. Barrington that you wish her to go to Professor Mannheim, let her go. She'll go anyhow. And you can't very well tell her you've changed your mind, can you? She'll take that merely as fear you're inconveniencing her, or at the worst, for rudeness on your part. No, Mrs. B. will go to the professor, that's all."

"What will happen, Faye?"

"Oh, it wil be unpleasant for him. And it will give her pleasure."

"And I will learn nothing, I suppose."

"No—you'll learn enough. Professor Mannheim after all liked Cliff very much."

Alma considered Faye's knowledge, then said, "Of course they were neighbors."

"Of course. And I don't think the professor holds anything against you Alma, over property reimbursement. And you're after all Cliff's aunt. You could even go to him later when all this blows over."

"When what blows over?"

"Oh, Mrs. Barrington's visit and any fuss that may ensue."

"Drink your coffee, dear, it's just freshly made."

Faye picked up her cup and stared at it, then sipped a bit.

"I don't know why I let Boyd persuade me to think she was the one to go to the professor for me. I can see I've put my foot in it."

"Don't blame yourself," Faye said with a strange serene kind of sweetness foreign to her old manner. "What will be, will be."

Alma studied the insipid intensity of Faye's expression.

"Faye, for God's sake, you're not going into Science!" Alma could not restrain her outburst.

Faye turned her face away. Her hand trembled so violently that the cup and saucer would have fallen from her hands had not Alma taken them.

"Poor child," Alma touched Faye's hair and then brought her head in an embrace against herself.

"There doesn't seem to be anything else, Alma," Faye's tear-choked voice spoke against the hollowness of her friend's bosom.

"It's all right, sweetheart," Alma spoke to her now in hushed tones. "It will *all* be all right. I'm not blaming you for a thing, see. Forgive me if I seemed to. You're overtired and need rest."

Alarmed even more by Faye's sudden emotional collapse

than her imminent conversion to Christian Science, Alma accompanied her friend home. Arm in arm they entered the house together.

In the front parlor, Faye listened intently and by a gesture with her hand admonished Alma not to raise her voice.

From the library beyond the parlor one could hear the TV set going at deafening volume, punctuated by oases of dead silence.

"Mother seems to be alone," Faye whispered.

Alma made no comment.

"Come with me," Faye implored Alma.

Mrs. Laird was alone as the two women entered the library. She had on a kind of morning cap which women had sometimes worn in Rainbow a generation or two ago, and which she had taken lately to affecting again. On the TV screen a woman with immense spectacles was lecturing on "Peoples of the World, a Symposium for the Woman at Home."

Mrs. Laird looked up heavily from her nap.

"Who have you got with you there?" she inquired, not covering her yawn, her voice blurred and expressionless like the television lecturer's.

"Mother, you certainly recognize Alma now," Faye chided the old woman. "Our neighbor for thirty years." As she spoke, Faye walked over to the TV set and toned down the volume.

"That's no more Alma than the man-in-the-moon," Mrs. Laird scolded. "Why do you fib to me when I have always seen through every one of your lies from the beginning? She's never been a truthful daughter," Mrs. Laird turned to Alma. "Sneaky through and through. If I hadn't watched her night and day years ago, she would have brought criminal disgrace on all of us. No control of her instincts."

"Mother, has Clare Himbaugh gone home?"

"I hope so," Mrs. Laird scolded. "The only reason she comes here is to get a free handout. She eat up all the candies and cookies the Eastern Star girls made for me. Picked clean that whole lovely Decoration Day gift of goodies you see over there—" Mrs. Laird waved to a gayly colored box on an end-table. "Then after she eats me out of house and home, she goes into my powder room there which was put in just for my own use because I have been so ill, and she makes everything untidy, throws my lovely hand-embroidered face towels on the floor, and is too dog-gone lazy to pull the chain on the toilet. Of course she's not in our class, and you have to overlook a good deal in her that way. Her mother was never married, you know."

"Oh, Mother," Faye protested, giggling mechanically.

"But that is no more Alma Mason than it is my great-aunt Ida. Why in creation you want to lie to me, Faye, when you know you won't get away with it, beats me."

Mrs. Laird adjusted her reading glasses and gazed studiously at the TV screen.

"Who is that terrible-looking woman talking at us now?" Mrs. Laird peered harder. "Anyone with a face that homely shouldn't be allowed in public view. Have you ever noticed that the uglier they come the more uplifted and important they make themselves out to be? This woman could be a nigger with that mouth and hair."

Faye turned off the set.

"You forget that I knew Alma Mason and her mother both very well," Mrs. Laird continued. "Her mother was a great woman, but Alma could never do anything right and so she bossed everybody, telling them how to do things right. It was her only accomplishment. She bossed from morning to night. I hope she's satisfied at the mess she made of her life, and the mess she made of her brother's too. Then she had some young nephew boarding with her, but it's just as well he went and got himself killed in the war, if you ask me . . ."

"But Mother, darling," Faye made a kind of whistling sound with her words, "you talk as if Alma were not right here in the room with us."

Alma felt that Faye spoke with more calm composure than she had a right to, considering the tone and nature of Mrs. Laird's remarks, but then she realized that Faye must be inured to these "attacks" from which the old woman suffered.

"How could Alma Mason be in this room when everybody knows she's in jail?" Mrs. Laird laughed, shaking her head.

Seeing the look of pain on her daughter's face, the mother added with condescending pedagogic impatience:

"Alma was to all intents and purposes a wife to her own brother, I think you're old enough to know such a thing, and they finally had to lock her up . . . But I suppose you've forgotten, it was ages ago."

"Let's go back into the parlor, for pity's sake," Faye cried, taking Alma's hand firmly. "Go back to your TV, Mother, like a good girl now," and she waited until her mother turned on the set.

Looking back, however, Alma gazed with an indeterminate expression at Mrs. Laird.

"Come, come," Faye begged her. "Don't take a word she

67

says seriously. She's obsessed with things that could never happen."

Alma, nevertheless, did not recover her composure quite so easily as Faye had apparently recovered hers, if indeed the latter could be said to have lost it.

"Just try to remember Mother's mental condition," Faye mumbled, "and think how mortified she would be if she knew what she was saying. And if you think what she said about you is bad, Alma, oh God, you ought to hear what she accused me of. I'd make the whore of Babylon a plaster saint."

"I've never seen her this bad before," Alma managed to remark. "It's you, though, I worry about." She took both Faye's hands in hers.

At that moment shots rang out from the TV screen, a horse whinnied, cries of older men were raised, and a pane of glass, perforated by bullets, fell to the mud of a frontier town.

"Kill all those good-for-nothing rotters!" Mrs. Laird's voice rose above the machine's crescendo. "Shoot to kill or you'll regret it later."

Faye's hands shook, she disengaged herself from Alma, and lit a Camel.

"It'd be a better world, you can believe me, if they killed more of the no-good rotters that are running this world to-day. You can quote me on that, too, girls. I was never afraid of a fight." Mrs. Laird's voice rose higher and higher drowning out now all but the gunfire sounds. "There's too many rotters around today and they've got to be done away with, that's what. They've got right into where you would never expect to find them, our schools and churches and lodges, the rotters are everywhere, and there's only one way to get them out: shoot to kill."

More gunfire rocked the TV set as Federal troops marched on the frontier town to rescue those imperilled by the outlaws.

"Shoot to kill!" Mrs. Laird's voice was supreme now even among the gunshots.

Then as the noise of bullets was dying down, they could hear the old woman cry softly:

"Faye, come in here and watch. They are raising the American flag. Old Glory. Doesn't it make your heart beat faster to see our flag, Faye? Come in here, dear, and salute the flag with me, and get your mind out of the gutter reading those books and papers. Do you hear me, Faye? Come in here with your mother and salute the flag."

A moment later they could hear her intoning as a Sousa march was played.

"Yes, yes," Faye laughed, and she offered Alma a Camel from her freshly-opened pack, forgetting for the hundredth time that Alma did not smoke.

MRS. B. AND BOYD

8

"I'VE been wanting to see you, Boyd Mason, for too long a time to dare think about." As Mrs. Barrington advanced toward Alma's brother, she motioned to a huge plant in a large jar near the front screen door. "Watch that awful cactus there. We keep it to discourage burglars when I'm gone and when I'm back nobody thinks to move it, as you can see."

Boyd's and Mrs. Barrington's entrance into the house sent scattering to the back rooms two maids and the man who acted as chauffeur and butler.

Mrs. B. ushered her visitor to a large chair covered with embossed peacocks. She took his straw hat and placed it underneath a white flowering plant which hovered over them from its base on an unfinished oak table.

"Here we've lived on Peninsula Drive across from each other for fifty years or more—and we never see each other," she cried, sitting down on a sofa on which she could manage her artificial foot with more grace than on an ordinary chair. "That's what the mid-century has brought to us, exits and entrances and never being anywhere!"

One of the maids who had vanished appeared now with a cup of hot chocolate.

"I thought you could stand with a taste of this," Mrs. B. told Boyd, motioning to the chocolate.

He beamed at her and Mrs. B. gave her satisfied proprietary smile.

The maid vanished again.

"I see Alma scurrying about from time to time, but I must say she never gives a look over here. I suppose she just thinks I'm gone all the time, so why look over, and God knows she's right. I don't know why I can't stay home."

"We both marvel at it," Boyd assured her, tucking his napkin in his vest.

"You marvel at my pep, I suppose, but I don't see how anybody could approve of all these trips I make, for I don't, but somehow—well, it's the mid-century, Boyd, that's all. We didn't use to live like his. *Then* we had everything where we were, but *now* there doesn't seem to be anything quite anywhere, and we keep flying like chickens without their heads all over *nowhere.*"

Boyd grinned and nodded, his napkin loosened and fell to the seat of his chair, and he picked it up again, and tucked it back more firmly into his vest.

Mrs. B's eye fell on a raveling which now lay across Boyd's trouser leg, fallen no doubt from his struggle with her linen napkin.

"To tell you the truth," Mrs. B. looked into her cup, "I've had Alma on my mind of late."

Boyd thanked her with a nod and a loud sip of chocolate.

"Do you know I couldn't sleep the other night for thinking about her. Retirement must be a terrible thing for a girl with her disposition."

Boyd cocked his head in the guise of one who considers this for the first time.

"It couldn't help be a terrible thing for her," Mrs. Barrington scotched any doubts on that score.

"Alma's restless," Boyd admitted. "And with more energy and plans than she knows what to do with."

Mrs. Barrington laughed cautiously but appreciatively.

"Well, I could have told her that a gift shop wouldn't use up all of her energy," Mrs. Barrington seemed to explain her own laugh. "Retirement will be harder on her than on almost anybody else ... And your yard, your lawn ... well, it's not the answer," Mrs. Barrington thought better than to discuss Alma and Boyd's yard. "Alma never cared too much anyhow about flowers and shrubs, now did she?"

Boyd did not comment.

"I think the reason that I could not sleep for thinking about her," Mrs. Barrington began again, "was something I heard from a very good friend of you both—it wasn't tale-bearing, I can assure you, so rest easy on that point."

Boyd looked blank for he could not think of anything in recent memory about which anyone could carry tales about him and Alma.

"This person told me Alma was writing a *memorial* to Cliff," Mrs. Barrington's voice moved somewhere between shock and disbelief, disappointment and stoic preparation for the worst.

"Oh, she's fiddling with something of the sort," Boyd dismissed the matter with the judicious calm of one who saw the memorial in its proper, and very minor, place in the lives of everybody concerned.

"But she is writing something about him," Mrs. B. said.

"It's still, I'd say, an idea."

"But I was told ... she had a record book ... and that

she sat all day trying to write down a coherent biography of Cliff."

Boyd nodded.

"But your nephew's not dead, Boyd," Mrs. B. appealed over his judge-like impassivity.

"*Missing* is what the Government told us."

"Then why in the name of God and common sense," and Mrs. Barrington waited for her voice to steady a bit, "why then does she want to write anything . . . until there's proof one way or the other?"

"I'm afraid I'm a bit to blame in encouraging her there . . ."

"Boyd, don't try to shoulder that responsibility," Mrs. B. laughed. "I know she wouldn't take your idea to do anything, or my idea or anybody's. She only does what she wants. That's why I admire Alma, I suppose. But a memorial—God in Heaven!"

"Cliff was her whole life after our mother died," Boyd said.

Mrs. B. indicated by a sudden rearranging of herself on the sofa that the *why* of Alma's predicament did not need to occupy their attention.

"I'll see Alma, of course," Mrs. B. cut him off. "But I wanted to get it straight from you what was going on before I went to her. I couldn't take even the best-intentioned second-hand report. And Mrs. Van Tassel, of course, is well-intentioned, though I'm afraid she's not much else . . . And she's taken to mumbling, too. One can hardly hear anything she says."

Boyd expressed some mild surprise that Mrs. B's informant had been Mrs. Van Tassel. He had settled on Faye Laird as the news-bearer.

"Writing down everything about a boy's life, great Scott," Mrs. B. shook her head.

"Oh, there's more to it even than you suspect," Boyd remembered his own promise to bring up the question of Professor Mannheim.

"Boyd Mason!" Mrs. B. said, ready to hear more in her severe role of arbiter.

"I mean, Alma herself has more or less asked me to ask you a favor."

"Yes."

"You see, contrary to what you may have heard, she hasn't written a line about Cliff that I know of. She's discovered there isn't a thing she knows for sure about him."

"And she had to buy a record book at the stationer's to learn that!" Mrs. B.'s laugh filled the room.

"But she's so set on writing something she has just

about made up her mind to go to Professor Mannheim for some assistance ..."

"Professor Mannheim?" Mrs. Barrington's teeth rattled as they did only when she was both terribly surprised and unprepared.

"He was a neighbor of ours, you remember."

"What has that got to do with Cliff?"

"Professor Mannheim was close to Cliff," and as he said this Boyd recognized that he had said something, the truth of which he had just now perceived.

"Boyd, please," Mrs. B. contradicted. "He was not close to Cliff. Mannheim taught him, of course, there was nothing we could do to prevent that ... Why, Willard Baker was closer to Cliff than Mannheim!" she sputtered.

Boyd stared at her coolly.

"All Cliff's other professors are gone, or dead," Boyd pointed out.

"That doesn't surprise me," Mrs. Barrington flared up. "The college can't keep a decent instructor, and as you say, they either die or leave."

"Alma didn't want to go to Professor Mannheim, and it was me suggested you might go for her. I'm afraid I've made you both uncomfortable."

"Rubbish," Mrs. B. said, and she rose. Seeing Boyd about to rise also, with a gesture she forbade him to follow her example.

"I always walk up and down when I'm thinking," she told him. "Of course I see as well as you do that Alma has to write this thing she's begun. She will never give up on anything that she has started, we all know that. But a memorial to a boy—who isn't even officially dead. Good God!

"And what would Mannheim know about an American boy?" she went on. "An old sitting-room pink of a past generation. What does he know about life, in fact? He was never a father himself. Sat around all his life talking about Europe and revolution and saving every cent he made here and investing it in the New York stock market while running down capitalism to his co-eds. I never even believed those scandals about him. I don't think he had the gumption to flirt with a co-ed, let alone lead her astray. He was too scared of his job. Professor Mannheim indeed."

Mrs. Barrington laughed at the peaked expression on Boyd's face.

"I'll see the old fool," she promised Boyd. "Will see him tomorrow if I can, and then the important thing will be to see Alma ... I'll talk some sense into that girl."

"I think what will happen, Mrs. Barrington—" Boyd

began, and he punctuated his remark by wiping his mouth with the linen napkin.

"Yes," Mrs. Barrington could not control her impatience. "What will happen in the end is that Alma will see there is nothing to write, and she'll stop."

"But we mustn't let her!" Mrs. Barrington sprang at him.

"I don't follow you. I thought——"

"No, Boyd, no. We mustn't let her fail, for pity's sake. She's never failed. She must write something and then have it mimeographed or printed somewhere, a few dozen copies. Otherwise there'll be no living with her. She'll dry up and blow away. Her gift shop isn't coming along, as any idiot can tell. And now the memorial. We must *find* her the material. We can find something. Then when she's written it, Boyd," and Mrs. B. clapped her hands sharply to call his attention to focus on her words, "*then* and then only, young man, can she forget it."

"It's so much fuss and feathers, Mrs. B.!"

"I wouldn't say that at all," she shook her head. "A loss like Cliff, at the very moment she retires. I can understand the whole thing. She must absolutely write the memorial . . . Of course I'll go to Mannheim. I'll have him over for tea, something dreadful like that. It will be grim even for him, I suppose, but I'd do anything for Alma."

"She won't forget this in you."

"What tomfoolery, Boyd. I'd do it for anybody decent."

Starting suddenly, Mrs. Barrington spoke as if she had hit on something:

"You know who would have some information, if you can call it that, would be Willard Baker, or that young man who takes care of his affairs, Vernon Miller. But Alma could go there herself . . ."

Boyd stared at her, and then, absent-mindedly perhaps, picked up his hat.

"You don't seem to agree with me, judging by your expression," she gibed.

"Willard Baker would never have occurred to me," Boyd said. "I don't know the other chap you refer to."

Mrs. Barrington said *hmm*, then, "I know what you're thinking, of course. Old Willard drinks and everything, but he does and did know young people. Talked to them by the hour. Cliff was no exception."

"News to me," Boyd mumbled, and he controlled his impulse to put on his hat.

"Willard used to see Cliff at my house, Boyd, in the days when I had those tiresome musical evenings—you remember, the baritone, and the pianist, and the harpist, and the rest that we brought in . . . You would never come."

74

"I was away on business a good deal in those years."

Mrs. B. nodded gravely.

"Willard can wait, of course," the old monarch said. "One thing at a time, and right now it's the professor."

Boyd sniggered in spite of himself, and Mrs. B. smiled.

"Now tell Alma to quit worrying and get herself over here. I must see and talk with that girl."

Boyd looked down, somewhat sheepishly, fingering the trade mark in the crown of his straw hat.

"I was never one of those fools who say that Alma should have been married, you know," she went on. "I really don't think Alma would have cared for any part of marriage. Though why a good-looking boy like you never re-married, Boyd Mason, I'll never know," and Mrs. B. gave him a tap as a kind of relief from their worrisome talk about his sister.

Pleased, Boyd took her hand. "Can't think about marriage when you're crowding a hundred," he joked.

"Boyd, I'll tell you a secret. I've been happier in many ways in my widowhood. Do you suppose God will strike me dead for saying that? I'm a selfish old gadabout, and there's no use fighting it."

They both laughed uproariously.

"It's always good to talk with a smart woman," Boyd told her, as she held open the screen door for him, and again warned with her finger against stumbling over the cactus.

"Don't stay away so long again," Mrs. B. urged, forgetting perhaps that he had not made the call on her, and that it was she who had asked him in.

"My love now to Alma, and remember she's not to worry," Mrs. B.'s voice came from behind the screen, too faint now to reach his deafness.

9

THE night of the day of Faye's talk with Alma and Boyd's with Mrs. B. was unusually humid and hot, pervaded by the smell of ketchup.

Leaving her mother in the care of her night-nurse, a colored woman who drove over from Sugar Ridge, Faye walked out of the house north down Crest Ridge Road.

From across the street she could see Willard Baker and his young companion, Vernon Miller, in their white tropical suits and between them Willard's inextinguishable cigar burning with unusual depth and redness. Faye imagined she could smell the cigar from her side of the street, through the heat and ketchup.

She had nearly got out of earshot when Willard's gentle but commanding voice said, "Faye, come over here and talk to two lonesome bachelors, like a good girl."

She was about to think up an excuse—she did want to walk off the pressures of the day—when suddenly even the energy to think up an alibi seemed more difficult than to comply with his request.

Faye walked over to the sprawling front porch, not having answered Willard, and nodded a greeting to the two men.

Even in the dark one could not help being struck by the beauty and excellence of Willard's and Vernon's clothes. Nobody else in Rainbow Center had ever dressed this expensively among the men or even, perhaps, among the women. Of the two, Vernon was the more tastefully dressed; he could have been a model. Willard, as usual, looked a bit ruffled, and some cigar ash had fallen on his lapel.

Two tall drinks sat on the small end table beside them.

"I know you won't have a drink or I'd offer you one," Willard said, getting up with some effort to greet her.

Vernon rose in a posture of shy awkwardness, incongruous with his clothes.

"I wouldn't mind a Cuba libre," Faye replied.

Willard pulled out a chair with a thick cushion on it for her, and motioning to his friend said:

"Vernon, will you do the honors?"

Vernon paused for a moment, as if not quite understanding Willard's question, and then with a trace of a sulk, went out into the kitchen for Faye's drink.

"I'm so glad you came up," Willard told her. "The heat is unmerciful. And that stink of cooking tomatoes!"

Faye nodded.

"You don't mind sitting here in public with two old soaks now?" Willard put his hand, in a paternal gesture of reassurance, on her knee.

Faye laughed, her girlish nature asserted itself suddenly, and she sat back on the chair, relaxing.

"Is your mother any better?" Willard wondered.

Faye shook her head and looked away in the direction of Peninsula Drive on the corner of which in sudden but dim illumination she saw the living room of the Masons, where, at that precise moment, Boyd was entering the front door and Alma rising to meet him. He must have just come home from his real-estate office. In the dim light of their front room their white hair shone like phosphorus.

"Old Boyd and Alma," Willard commented drily, noticing where Faye's eyes had strayed.

Vernon Miller returned with Faye's Cuba libre.

"A coaster and a napkin before you sit down again, please," Willard told his friend with more than a slight edge in his voice.

Vernon's face flushed, he wheeled about quickly, and re-entered the house.

"What's this I hear about Alma writing a book about her nephew?" Willard inquired, and as he said this his attention was attracted by another deposit of ash falling from his cigar onto his jacket. He carefully flicked as much of the ash as he could from the cloth.

"Good heavens, it's not a book." Faye sipped her drink.

"Well, she's writing something, isn't she?" Willard snapped.

"Yes, of course," Faye said, but weariness seemed to prevent her from going on, and she accepted her coaster and napkin from Vernon Miller at that moment without thinking to thank him.

When Vernon stood on obsequiously at Faye's side for a moment longer, Willard gave him a peremptory nod to be seated.

"Faye," Willard began in his quiet soothing tones, "don't you take those trips to Europe you used to a few years back?" He looked at her now with real concern.

"A *few* years back, Willard!" She sipped at her drink. "That was fifteen years ago if it was a day," she reminded him.

"I think you could stand with a little bit of Europe again, if you ask me," Willard raised his glass to her.

She drank again.

"Vernon here has been coaxing me to go to Europe with him, but I won't hear of it. Once was enough for me, though I won't tell you how long ago that was. And anyhow everything European seems to be over here, and all the Americans are over there, so why not stay home and enjoy your own country to yourself."

Vernon Miller made a short swift sound of impatience.

"Don't you think Faye could stand with a little Europe, Vernon?" Willard inquired of his friend.

It was clear both from Willard's tone and the young man's sulking that they had been quarrelling, and Faye saw that she had probably been invited in only to forestall the continuation of unpleasantness.

Faye put her drink down noisily on its coaster.

"Is your Cuba libre all right?" Willard asked pointedly.

"It couldn't be better," Faye replied in an almost threateningly loud voice.

"Thank you, Faye," Vernon told her, gratefully. "I can always count on you."

Faye looked at him more closely. In the dim light of the porch his face seemed lacquered and made-up, and one could not tell whether he was 18 or 30.

"You shouldn't want to send me off on a boat to Europe when you don't want to go yourself, Willard," Faye broke the ominous silence.

"Maybe Faye and I should go to Europe together," Vernon said, considerably brightened by what must have been a long swig in the kitchen.

"That's an idea," Faye replied, feeling a bit gay from her drink.

"What will you use for money?" Willard turned almost savagely to his friend.

There was a moment of strained silence, then Faye cried: "We'll use my teacher's retirement insurance, won't we, Vernon?"

The young man swallowed hard, and then, after a struggle said, "That's right, Faye."

"She's Professor Laird to the likes of you," Willard remarked, but his voice was less unpleasant now, even though he had meant his remark to be cutting.

"Willard is going to tell you in a minute how I never finished the eighth grade," Vernon said softly to Faye.

"I never said you weren't bright," Willard warned.

"I think you're lucky to have Vernon," Faye said, perhaps to her own surprise.

"Well, Faye Vernon and I are both even-tempered people. We quarrel all the time."

Willard laughed, Faye sniggered bashfully, and Vernon, now completely relaxed by rum, sank back into his makeshift deck-chair and lit a long cigarette with an enamel tip.

"I am curious all the same to know what in hell Alma is writing about her nephew," Willard returned to this topic.

"That will be some book," Vernon sat up briefly with a knowing expression.

"I'd forgotten that you knew Cliff, Vernon," Faye revived a bit more.

"He didn't know him from Adam," Willard scoffed, then shifted violently in his seat as some hot cigar ash fell across his hand.

"I knew Cliff fairly well," Vernon pretended to ignore Willard's comment. "We used to talk together in the yard— over there by the old snow-ball bush. Cliff was always out in the yard. I don't think he liked to be inside with his aunt and uncle."

"I don't know how you or anybody else could say you knew Cliff Mason," Willard remarked. "He couldn't talk, for one thing, unless he was repeating his schoolwork. He was what they now call, I understand, non-verbal."

"He could talk when he wanted to," Vernon remarked softly, whether to prolong the argument or whether perhaps he knew something about Cliff nobody else knew.

"All right, tell us, smarty, what he told you," Willard remarked, when a heavy burst of coughing silenced him from saying more. His cough was so violent that Faye and Vernon exchanged looks of uneasiness.

Recovering at last, and sipping his drink superciliously, Willard proceeded: "The Masons's nephew had had everything taken out of him from bossing," he said. "He must have been bossed from the time he emerged from the womb. Getting killed in the army probably was a relief to him."

"He's missing, not killed," Faye said insipidly, like a young girl who repeats a phrase brought home to her many times.

"Missing *is* killed, Faye dear, in army talk. Cliff's dead."

"On the contrary, Willard, I think Cliff will be back," Faye spoke dreamily, and she looked down at her drink, which she had finished.

"Get up and get Faye another Cuba libre," Willard turned to Vernon Miller.

"I'm not quite ready for one," Faye was emphatic.

"When you are, whistle," Willard told her. "Vernon loves to wait on ladies."

"That is so terribly true," Vernon stared wide-eyed at Willard until the latter lowered his eyes.

"Old Alma must be losing some of her marbles," Willard went on, a bit more subdued. "Writing a book about her nephew! At her age."

"Retirement is hard for Alma," Faye seemed to be reminding herself of the problem.

"She's got nobody to boss now," Willard said. "Except old Boyd, and I don't think she can find much left in him any more to really chew on. He's deaf, too, fortunately." He laughed after saying this.

"Cliff was the loneliest boy I think I ever knew, outside of maybe me," Vernon said suddenly and his remark, directed to nobody in particular, gave the effect, at that moment, of having been flashed before them in large letters on a TV screen.

"I never thought that about him," Faye mused in a sleepy voice.

"Believe me, he could talk," Vernon said. "But who the hell could he talk with, I ask you." He gulped.

"Obviously to great big-hearted understanding you," Willard addressed his friend with vicious incision.

Faye rose at this point, muttering an excuse that she must not leave her mother alone any longer.

Willard put a restraining hand on her arm. "It's too hot to sleep and there's too much smell of tomatoes even if the temperature were right. Be a good sport and have one more drink with us." Suddenly he looked out into the Mason's backyard and squinted.

"All Vernon and I will do," Willard went on, still looking inquiringly ahead of him, "is sit here and get drunk and say perfectly abominable things to one another. He may even have to kill me."

While Willard was speaking, Vernon had drawn very close to Faye and then quickly, almost imperceptibly, he touched his hand on her waist, allowing it to rest there. She made no move to disengage herself.

Willard turned suddenly from his staring in front of him to catch sight of Vernon's closeness to Faye, but restraining an impulse to say something, he gazed again at his object of attention in the Masons's backyard.

"Look, you two," Willard said, "isn't that old Alma herself out there in the garden, walking around like a goblin? Look where I'm pointing."

Faye walked a step or two away from Vernon, and fixed her gaze where Willard had directed. "It's Alma all right," she agreed, worried.

"Let's ask her up for a drink," Willard suggested.

"Oh God in heaven, no!" Faye expostulated. "You must know by now how Alma feels about drinking," and she glanced down at her own glass.

"Why not invite her," Willard said. "I don't think she's ever met Vernon, for one thing," and his voice had an edge. "She's always off teaching the fifth grade in Mt. Gilead or somewhere. I'm going to ask her up—if you love-birds will excuse me," he added.

Hobbling down the front porch steps, and sauntering out into the yard, Willard reached the plot of ground which separated the two properties, and called out Alma's name softly.

The aunt turned round, surprised as much at the sound of her own name as at the sight of Willard Baker coming toward her. Faye and Vernon watched her advance nervously to meet Willard. They could only faintly hear her voice, and his rejoinder of "Oh come and join the party!"

While Alma and Willard talked, Vernon had drawn close to Faye again and he kissed her now on the hair.

"Why did you have to let him see us together and spoil things," she cried, but there was no real irritation or anger in her tone.

He took hold of her hand.

"Before he comes back," Vernon began, "what time can I see you tomorrow?"

"I don't think we should see one another again," she told him, removing her hand from his.

"Is it your mother again?" he spoke with boredom and cold anger.

The loud belly-laugh of Willard Baker resounded throughout the neighborhood.

"He is bringing Alma up here," Faye said, this time not resisting the pressure from Vernon's hand.

"What time can I see you tomorrow?" he begged her.

"Come over at ten," she replied.

Breaking away from Vernon, Faye walked over to the front steps and greeted Alma, who looked like the one who bore all the guilt and blame, putting her hands to her hair awkwardly.

"I was just explaining to Willard," Alma took Faye's hand, "I was scarcely expecting company—indoors or out." She looked down at her thin white dressing gown in grave concern.

"Will you bring a nice cold drink for Miss Mason?" Willard spoke to Vernon. Then with sudden affected thoughtfulness, Willard addressed Alma: "You've met my man Friday, I believe, Vernon Miller."

The older man seemed suddenly drunk.

"No, I'm afraid I haven't had the pleasure," Alma replied, looking at Vernon.

"Then introductions are in order," Willard said in a stentorian voice. "Vernon was a bosom-friend of your nephew, Cliff," he declared.

Alma extended her hand to Vernon and gave him unaccountably a long searching look unlike any that Faye could ever remember seeing on the old woman's face.

Vernon expressed his pleasure in meeting Alma and then asked, "What kind of a drink would you enjoy, Miss Mason?"

"Oh, Willard is just joking about my drink, Mr. Miller," Alma pointed out to him. "He knows I don't touch the stuff," and she laughed in extenuation of Willard's invitation.

"You've got to have a drink now, Alma, and I'm not going to let you go home without one," Willard came up to her, putting his arm about her waist, perhaps in derisive imitation of Vernon's embracing of Faye. "We front-families have to set an example," he added.

Exchanging a look of understanding with Alma, Vernon asked her:

"What can I bring you to drink?"

"Oh, whatever it is Faye's having," Alma replied airily.

"That's the spirit," Willard remarked, as Vernon left the room to prepare the drink.

Following an awkward silence after the young man's leaving, Willard began, "Vernon and I are off to Michigan in a few days now."

"Some hunting and fishing?" Alma wondered, holding her wrapper carefully about her throat.

"We'll just loll and loaf, since you ask me," Willard replied. "And inhale some uncontaminated air from the woods and streams."

Alma nodded, considering this carefully, and was about to make some comment when Willard exclaimed, evidently in genuine relief, "Ah, here is our man-servant back already!" as Vernon came through the screen door carrying a tray with a pitcher and some glasses.

"I made fresh drinks for everyone, and a special concoction for Miss Mason," Vernon informed them, and he winked surreptitiously at the aunt.

"Where's Miss Mason's napkin?" Willard demanded sharply, and he gave the sudden impression again of extreme intoxication and anger.

"Oh, I don't need such a thing at all," Alma retorted, managing to put down for the moment Willard's edge of ill-temper.

They all sat drinking now with the exception of Alma,

who having tasted from her glass gingerly, only made pretense from then on to imbibe any more.

"Well, I wonder where we'll all be a year from this summer!" Willard exclaimed, raising his glass in the manner of a toast.

He sank back now in his chair, put his glass down, drained, and it was clear to all, with the possible exception of Alma, that he was at the stage of his drinking when he would either go to sleep or be sick.

"Do you suppose they make ketchup in hell?" Willard inquired suddenly, half-rousing himself from his stupor.

Everybody laughed in spite of the unpleasantness of his expression.

"You haven't received any new word about Cliff?" Vernon addressed himself to Alma in the silence that followed Willard's last remark.

"Not recently," Alma said with sudden brightness. "But of course we expect to hear."

Vernon nodded.

"I didn't know you knew Cliff at all, until Willard remarked on it here this evening," Alma spoke with bashful, agreeable surprise.

Vernon did not reply, his eyes on Willard, perhaps to determine if he was asleep.

"I think we two ladies must be leaving," Faye spoke at last, her eyes also uneasily on Willard.

"And when I have just made Mr. Miller's acquaintance!" Alma cried gaily. She rose even as she said this, and it was clear that although she had been pleased to meet Vernon, she was also eager to leave Willard Baker.

Vernon assisted the ladies down the front steps into the yard, and they stood for a few more minutes whispering together, out of earshot of the porch. Then saying goodnight they wandered off in separate directions.

"Where in hell have you been all this time?" Willard chided when Vernon came back on the porch. The older man acted both sober and wide-awake.

Vernon explained that he had shown the ladies home.

Willard snorted, then said, "Well, you made a fine show of yourself tonight."

"I didn't pass out at least," Vernon retorted.

"The way you kept pawing at old Faye Laird was enough to make anybody vomit—let alone pass out. Well, if it's *her* money you're after now, let me tell you something. Old Mrs. Laird has willed all of that to churches and lodges. Her daughter will hardly inherit enough to live on . . . and the old woman left it that way so Faye won't marry."

"Thanks for the advice, Willard. I'll drop Faye at once, of course."

"You'll drop her, that's right, or you'll get out of my house. What the hell do you mean making love to her in front of my very eyes, in my own home."

Vernon finished the rest of his drink.

"And quit drinking so much," Willard began again. "In the first place, I'm not that well-off—to run a private bar for you, and in the second place, you'll be getting fat and blubbery."

"That's from the horse's mouth, I guess," Vernon retorted.

"And what's this goddam talk about how you knew Cliff Mason!" Willard fumed.

"Because I did," Vernon stood up to him quietly. "As much as you let me know anybody, I might say."

"Go ahead with your speech about how I've ruined your life."

Then musing on in studied bitterness, Willard said, "I suppose that you've decided to make up this story about Cliff Mason so that you can get into old Aunt Alma's good graces, too. That's about it. Always looking around for a future port-in-a-storm. Don't think I didn't see you making up to the old bag."

"Well, who the Christ invited her up here in the first place?" Vernon shot back, with a kind of apathetic rage.

"That was a mistake," Willard agreed. "I should never introduce you to anybody. God, if my family could only see me now," and he seemed to appeal to all that was highest and supreme in the nature of things.

"They wouldn't b͏ too surprised," Vernon mumbled.

"What did you say?" Willard fumed.

"You heard me."

"How could you understand anything about my family?" Willard looked at his friend with open eyes. "A bastard without any name of his own like you talking about my family when the very mention of *Baker* in this part of the country has been enough to open all doors."

They sat on in their savage silence and contempt for some minutes.

Then trembling, Willard summoned all his strength to command, saying:

"You can pack and get out, do you hear? Tonight. Go right upstairs and gather your things together and get out. You've had your last handout here."

Vernon rose, put his glass down with steady deliberateness, and walked toward the screen door.

At the same moment, Willard made a feeble attempt to rise, crying out, "Where are you going?"

"I'm packing and getting out like you told me."

"Sit down." Willard spoke between entreaty and command.

Vernon remained standing, his hand on the delicate glass knob of the screen door.

"I'm sorry," Willard shouted.

"Yes, I know," Vernon replied with icy boredom.

"I said I'm sorry," Willard repeated, looking up, imploring, at his friend. "Please sit down." The older man began to weep softly. "Vernon," he said, "I'm not well. . . . Please," and he motioned for his friend to sit down.

Vernon walked slowly, in the mechanical manner of one who answers a telephone which rings continuously, and took his accustomed chair beside his companion. He patted the older man's hand, absentmindedly.

"Do try to be understanding," Willard begged. "For God's sake, try."

"Don't persecute yourself," Vernon said.

"You've meant more to me than my family ever did." Willard grasped the boy's hand. "You've given me the only happiness I think I ever had. I don't know why I say such terrible things to you."

"I think you should see a doctor, Willard."

"I've been with doctors all my life. That's what's wrong with me."

Vernon continued to pat and smooth his friend's fat trembling hand with weary affection and patient concern.

"No matter what I ever say to you, Vernon," Willard held his friend's hand in his, "remember you're all I have. Don't ever leave me. I've put down everything in writing. You don't have to worry about the future after I'm gone . . . You're all I have or need."

FOUR THOUSAND DOLLARS

10

AFTER Boyd Mason had left Mrs. Barrington's house for his real-estate office, the old monarch sat down at her spinet writing desk and in her model Spencerian hand composed two notes, the first to Professor Mannheim, the second to Alma Mason. They were delivered the first thing the next morning by her chauffeur and factotum, Ed Shaeffer.

The notes, almost identical in content, differed greatly in tone, the one to Professor Mannheim reading like an official summons to court, while the message to Alma, although peremptory, was couched in terms of friendship and sentiment.

Neither Alma nor Mrs. Barrington would have been able to understand the effect of the note on Professor Mannheim. They were, after all, in and of Rainbow for life, and though the professor had lived in the community for half his chronological age he was, if anything, more ill-at-ease and insecure than when he had arrived as a young man. He saw in Mrs. Barrington's communication the hint of every threat and disaster which he had feared from her and the college for all his years of sojourn here.

It was a warm morning when Ed Shaeffer put the note into the professor's hands, and it promised to be a scorcher. Professor Mannheim had planned to do very little this day, not only because of the weather, but because it marked the anniversary of something which he hugged to himself in secret—today was the anniversary of his first wife's death, and he had planned, as always, and unbeknownst to the second Mrs. Mannheim, to go to the tiny Jewish cemetery some ten miles out of town and visit her grave.

He could think of nothing now but his command visit to Mrs. Barrington. She was, in his eyes, a much more formidable figure than the President of the college, for the latter based his judgment of a faculty member on such simple principles as church membership and community participation, speaking engagements before the Kiwanis and Rotary, and frequent attendance at football banquets and college homecomings. Having failed to meet these requirements, Professor Mannheim could expect indifference and even contempt from the President and consequently from the board of trustees, but at the same time he could count on being tolerated as an associate professor until retirement provided, of course, his behavior or opinions did not arouse comment and that he did not broach the subject of promotion.

But Mrs. Barrington, Professor Mannheim knew, disapproved of him at every level of his being. His being a Jew was the least of it here, and his political opinions—which he now never uttered—and his books were less unacceptable than the way he wore his clothes and spoke English. Mrs. Barrington could not reconcile what he *was*, in face, with what she thought a life-long resident of Rainbow and the college campus should be.

Walking up and down his study with the note held in his hand, remembering that he was 60 and in five years would be retired, he kept saying to himself that whatever he had done or not done, the board of trustees could hardly dismiss him at this late date, no matter what power Mrs. Barrington might yield.

Yet the terror of the note did not leave him. As he stood alone in his study, thick hard tears that seemed to wound the eye fell upon the carpet bringing to mind his wife's death and the tears he had shed at that time, which had fallen easily, softening his grief. In all his life he had never felt so alone, but this time he was alone as an old man. The strength he had always been able to summon in the past was gone, like his easy tears, and he felt something cold and intolerable sweep across him like the wing of the angel of death.

Disturbed by her husband's closeting himself in his study for such a long time, Rosa Mannheim walked in upon him and, surprised at his sorrow, attempted to say something comforting. Looking at her suddenly, he only saw that she was somehow not with him, whether because she had been born in Rainbow of a background and manner too different from him, or merely because he was too old and tired now to have anybody stand with him as his equal in affliction.

"If they fire me, Rosa, they will fire me," he told her. "I can't fight the spirit of a community."

"In this day and age?" he heard his wife say. "They would not dare."

He took her hand in his and kissed it, but his tears frightened her, and he felt her hand tense in his, as if she wanted to draw back.

Professor Mannheim therefore looked both stiff and wilted that warm summer day when he paid his "command" call on Mrs. Barrington.

Mrs. Barrington was not as keenly aware of his existence

as the professor feared. He was more of a name to her than a person, a name annually brought to her attention when she attended the June meeting of the trustees. Years before, like everybody else, she had heard that he had been sexually loose with certain co-eds, but there had never been any proof and the President had not acted. As the years came and went, the rumors finally died down. Even when they were from time to time revived among the older alumni in the hiatus of conversation at a football banquet or homecoming, Professor Mannheim's recent excessive aging rather gave the lie to their ever having been true. Once permanently old, he had been taken for granted in the college community, if not as a fixture like the full professors, at least as a kind of perennial, and he and his articles on Marx and socialism were ignored, if not forgotten, by nearly everybody, town, gown, faculty wives, and trustees.

Though Rosa Mannheim had wept as she saw her husband go down the walk to his engagement, the professor himself, once he was out of his study, got back some of his old vim and assurance. He remembered momentarily, as he went up Mrs. Barrington's step, his former reputation of power with the fair sex.

"I must ask you to excuse me for bringing you clear over here on such an unmerciful day," Mrs. Barrington advanced with her ready cordiality to meet him, half-staring at his collar crushed with perspiration.

"How are you, Professor?" Her imperious question seemed to answer itself. She waved for the maid to prepare his chair in the next room.

Seeing the look of worried consternation on his face, and with a second critical glance at his collar, Mrs. Barrington, once they were seated for tea, went directly to the matter at hand.

"We'll not go about Robin Hood's barn," she said. "I've asked you here, Professor Mannheim, on a matter that concerns neither you nor me directly."

Professor Mannheim's face brightened, then darkened again, for he felt this sunny beginning was only a preparation for her coming work of devastation.

"It's our old friend Alma Mason, who'll be along in a minute, I hope." Mrs. Barrington looked up at the grandfather clock, which seemed to obey her glance at that instant, for it chimed.

She poured him a cup of tea, motioning away the maid, and looked questioningly at the sugar and the lemon and the cream. He indicated he took none of these, and accepted the cup from her. Then he changed his mind and took two lumps of sugar. At another glance from Mrs. B. he touched his collar awkwardly.

"You remember Alma—Cliff Mason's aunt, who helped raise him . . ."

"But of course, who could fail to remember!" he erupted, sputtering a bit from his quick sip of tea, his English sounding suddenly so foreign.

"I knew you would remember Cliff," Mrs. Barrington softened her gaze at him. "But I wanted to be sure before we talked," she finished rather loud and sharp.

"I remember Cliff as though it were today." Professor Mannheim acted mildly encouraged.

"Then you can help us," the old monarch cried. "Of course!" She laughed. "That is, you can help Alma," and her voice was again severe. "As to Cliff, well, I suspect he may be dead." She put her cup down.

"It would seem too good to be true, if after all these months he was alive," the professor nodded. "Still—!"

"He is undoubtedly dead, I suppose, Professor Mannheim. Or *worse.*"

The professor loosened his grip on his tea cup, and to avoid spilling it put it down hastily.

"She wants to write a memorial," Mrs. Barrington said coldly and she glanced at the clock out of the corner of her eye.

"A memorial to Cliff?"

"A biography." Mrs. B. recognized the justness of the professor's astonishment. "That's why I've inconvenienced you by asking you here." There was a trace of long-extinguished feminine coyness in her tone. "Alma doesn't know anything to write," she resumed her old firmness.

Professor Mannheim colored unaccountably.

"She didn't know her own nephew," Mrs. B. brought out.

Professor Mannheim nodded, meaning he understood this universal failing.

"Alma's brother—Boyd Mason—and I thought you might be able to tell us something about Cliff's academic career. Anything Alma could use in her memorial."

Professor Mannheim brightened visibly once he had reason to believe that his summons here this morning was a matter merely of writing the life of Cliff Mason, but at the words *academic career,* his face clouded over again.

Mrs. Barrington, noticing his hesitation, waited and in a moment she seemed to turn to frost.

"Cliff was only at the college a little over a year," the professor attempted to explain his sudden lack of readiness and enthusiasm for helping. "He did not distinguish himself, I'm afraid."

"I see," Mrs. Barrington said loftily.

"But by the very oddest chance," Professor Mannheim raised his voice in an attempt perhaps to sound cheerful, "while going through some of my old class files only last week, I came upon several examination papers, a theme or two, and my own *curriculum vitae* of young Cliff."

"Then we do have a beginning!" Mrs. B. cried in the manner of one clutching at a straw.

"But the very idea that his papers should have been the ones to survive, and of the other students of that period— not a trace!"

"Remarkable," Mrs. Barrington agreed but her mind, it was obvious, was not at the moment on the problem of Cliff and his papers or Alma and her book.

As a matter of fact, she was thinking of a luncheon at the Elks where she was due to appear in less than twenty minutes and give a speech.

"You will, of course, hand over the boy's papers to his aunt," Mrs. B. said rhetorically.

"That goes without saying," the professor nodded.

"I can't think what on earth is keeping Alma!" Mrs. Barrington stared with mild indignation at the grandfather clock. "She's an hour late."

Mopping his brow surreptitiously and quickly, Professor Mannheim turned to the subject at hand again: "I believe there was something about Cliff that might have proved exceptional," he mused.

Mrs. Barrington watched him.

"But it had not developed, you see," he sighed.

"One could hardly have expected it to at the age of eighteen," the old monarch commented with some dryness.

"Exactly," he hastened to agree. "Which is why the thought of writing a book about him struck me as—"

"*Absurd,*" Mrs. B.'s voice boomed. She nodded. "But it strikes you no more so than it does the rest of us," she reassured him. "The sense or nonsense of writing such a book is, however, not the point. The point is Alma. She's got to write the biography. She always has to finish everything she begins, and she's got the whole neighborhood, indeed the town, involved in her writing this plaguey memorial. We've got to push her to finish it so that she can go on ahead with something sensible. By then, she'll know her nephew is either dead or alive."

"Cliff lost his mother and father early in life, I recall," Professor Mannheim refreshed his own memory.

Mrs. Barrington nodded, adding, "Alma Mason took over from there. With what success, I will not try to pass judgment. She seems to me though, confidentially, to be the last person on earth God meant for a parent."

Before Professor Mannheim could reply to her statement, both he and the old monarch were startled a bit on hearing the doorbell ring.

As the maid ushered in Alma Mason, it was instantly clear that the latter had gone to a great deal of trouble getting herself up. She wore a new cotton print dress, perhaps a bit young for her, and a striking necklace, obviously not from her gift shop. She was also wearing, for the first time in Mrs. B.'s memory, just a hint of lipstick.

Although Professor Mannheim had been warned by his hostess that Alma was coming, he was visibly uncomfortable at the sight of Cliff's aunt. Alma, who had not dreamed of finding the professor here, stopped short in her tracks.

From her sofa, Mrs. B. studied their discomfiture.

"I wanted to surprise you, Alma," the old monarch smiled, giving at the same time an imperious look to the maid for more tea. "But of course you would have to be late for the professor."

"I never expected—" Alma babbled, confounded at Professor Mannheim's appearance and embarrassed at meeting him face to face. She believed she might have not recognized him without his hat, for he was now completely bald except for some untidy tufts of patriarchal white about the ears. His eyes had lost all their pride and warmth, and his jaw sagged like that of a man who has suffered recently a mild stroke.

"Of course you didn't, my dear," Mrs. B. interrupted. "But it's too late even to apologize. I'm nearly late myself for my speaking engagement at the Elks. But we have good news for you, Alma dear . . . The professor has found some things of Cliff's you may be able to use for your book . . . exams and compositions, and the like."

"You don't mean to tell me," Alma turned, constrained and radiant, to the professor. His own obvious discomfiture relieved in part some of Alma's own confusion and embarrassment.

From inside the next room the whir of a gigantic electric fan was heard, set in motion at a signal to the maid from Mrs. B., for the heat was becoming pronounced even under these courtroom-high ceilings.

"They're his papers and exams from world history, Miss Mason," Professor Mannheim explained, assuming his forensic manner for the first time since his arrival. "There may be something in them for you."

"How kind of you to keep them for such a long time." Alma's voice came to him somewhat obliquely, whirred as it were through the blades of the electric fan.

Alma accepted her cup of tea from the maid, smiling with a sweetness uncommon to her at home.

As there was continued silence from Mrs. Barrington on the sofa, Professor Mannheim, his face flushed from the heat, the exertion, the tea, and the sudden certainty that his sitting here with the two women did not involve him or his career, began a veritable cascade of words, based this time not on world history but college memories, memories of Cliff in particular.

"The one thing I will always remember about him," Professor Mannheim looked into the high ceiling, "the one thing I will always take away from thinking about him was the way he showed, in his face, how much he was expecting of life ... Yes, that was his distinguishing quality," he turned to Alma, "how much he was expecting ..."

The two women considered this.

Professor Mannheim talked on. On the gradual sensation of reprieve which had come to him, his English seemed another language in sound and pronunciation; his collar became completely drenched in sweat and opened a bit under his tie; and a trickle of tea found its way from his mouth to his coat lapel.

Suddenly he wept in short almost animal-like sobs.

Alma exchanged glances with Mrs. B., but the latter was as impassive and controlled as she had been in the years when she assembled young students to hear an unusual baritone or harpist in her music room. She even nodded, as if his weeping was after all what she had expected from him.

Dabbing his eyes with his handkerchief, and attempting to straighten his collar—he did not seem aware that the button of his shirt was undone—Professor Mannheim managed to repeat his offer to Alma to do all he could in helping her write the book on her nephew.

"Of course you will want to see one another again particularly about that—just the two of you," Mrs. Barrington's voice boomed with finality from the sofa. "But I felt you should be brought together first," she gave her only explanation for summoning them so unexpectedly this morning, and at the same time by her voice and manner, indicated that her time with them had run out.

The grandfather clock struck twelve.

"I will bring Cliff's papers and his *curriculum vitae* to you, Miss Mason," Professor Mannheim said. He stood up, perhaps galvanized by the glance which Mrs. B. gave him.

"I'm so terribly sorry to have been late." Alma also rose now, a bit slow in catching the old monarch's cue of dismissal.

"I would have you both stay on and on," Mrs. B. took hold of Alma's hand in rising. "But it's high noon and Ed Shaeffer has been waiting outside there in the car for a quarter of an hour. Did I say . . . I have to address a luncheon at the Elks, of all things, and in such weather."

Alma and Professor Mannheim babbled their sympathy and understanding.

"But you two may stay on here and talk to your heart's content," she informed them, and there could be no doubt that, though this was a sudden thought on her part, she meant it.

"I think the professor and I will wait until he can give me Cliff's papers," Alma backed out weakly.

He nodded energetic agreement.

"Just as you wish, my dear." Mrs. Barrington pressed Alma's hand in hers. Then turning to the professor, she said, "I can't thank you enough."

Tears still stood in his eyes but, as he expressed his thanks to her, it was his collar Mrs. B. was looking at.

They all said goodbye again on the front porch, and then took final and rather rapid leave of one another.

At home Rosa Mannheim had been waiting for her husband, in bleak resignation, walking up and down the line of geranium pots in her living room.

Seeing him toiling up the front walk, she opened the screen door wide, without addressing a word to him. Soon he was pacing up and down in the safety of his study, as he described his meeting with Mrs. Barrington and Alma Mason, while his wife sat half-facing him on the window-sill with the encyclopedias.

"Imagine her calling me up there over Cliff Mason!"

"Cliff Mason," Rosa exclaimed. "The boy who used to live next door to you."

"His aunt wants to write a book about him."

"Oh, no." she said. Studying her husband carefully, she added, "You look even worse than when you left. Are you sure it was just Cliff Mason they called you over there about?"

"Put aside once and for all any fears you may have about our security," he told her.

She made a gesture of irritability.

"I will be allowed to go on being an associate professor until I retire or die or they quit teaching world history . . . And we'll get our pension and all."

"You act sorry the old rip didn't tell you you were fired!" she retorted.

He shrugged his shoulders, then took out his German pipe and tasted it briefly.

"Cliff Mason must be dead," he spoke as if to himself.

"Cliff Mason!" She looked away with impatience and disgust. "There must be something more to this than you're telling me."

"I've told you the whole thing—ridiculous as it sounds."

"If we could only leave this God-awful community," Rosa implored.

"This morning brought back a whole wave of things I'd forgotten," Professor Mannheim confided. He bit on his pipe.

"Such as what," she wondered.

"Don't be so suspicious," he scolded now. "When I tell you there's nothing to fear, there's nothing to fear."

"Then why do you look as if you'd seen a ghost?" she flung the words at him.

"One forgets so much in the daily routine of living," he tried to explain. "Rosa, today was the anniversary of my first wife's death."

"I'm sorry," she said wearily.

"I don't look the way I do on account of that," he spoke with some of his old stamina. "The sight of those two de-sexed pillars of the American Revolution knocked the pins from under me, I guess . . . I must have behaved ridiculously."

"Why ridiculously?" She was breathless.

"I cried!" he shouted at her. "Wept before them like a baby!"

"Why do you torture me like this?" she came back to her original fear and suspicion. "I know something happened. You're doing a hell of a job preparing me for the worst, I'll say. But you've done a hell of a job by me all along, if you ask me."

He made no attempt to explain to her, and talked on as he would have talked, had he found himself alone in the study.

"As I say, being with those two old war-horses—it brought my whole life in this town back to me. The mention of Cliff, perhaps . . . I lived neighbors to the Masons, you remember, just before my first wife died."

"Of course I remember all that," she cried.

"You remember, too, that just before my wife passed away . . . that spring."

"I can't very well forget it," she said, anger and bitterness struggling with genuine sadness.

"Those last days, just before she died, we were having

94

that passionate love affair, you and I. I told you then it was the only passionate love affair of my life."

"And you've changed your mind about that, too, I suppose," she said, expressionless.

"I loved you intensely," he went on. "But I loved my wife then, too, I believe more than I had ever loved her before. How would a person explain that?"

"I don't know what in the name of God you are trying to tell me, or what happened to you at Mrs. Barrington's," she muttered, but she seemed calmer as she said this, and at the same time more indifferent toward him than ever before in their relationship.

He waited to light his pipe, and she watched him as he painstakingly made the first draw on it.

"I was so beside myself the week she died," the professor went on. "I had to talk to somebody."

"I wasn't enough," she said.

"I had to talk to somebody—outside it all."

"And you talked to Cliff Mason."

"How did you guess that?" He sucked on the pipe.

"Isn't that where you're naturally leading—if you're leading anywhere?" she cried. "You can never say a thing straight out. No, you have to wind and turn and turn and wind until one is worn out and crazy waiting for you to come to the point. Well, why not? It's your profession, talking."

"I did tell Cliff Mason," he went on.

"And he kept your secret."

"I have no reason to suppose he didn't. Right afterwards he went to Korea. And if Cliff hadn't listened to me the day he did—whether he understood what I said to him or not is beside the point—I think, yes I do think I might have done away with myself. I had the gun."

Rosa looked into her extended open palms, but he knew she listened to what he had just said with more acceptance than anything he had told her in years. If she no longer loved him, if as he suspected she sometimes hated him, perhaps at this moment at least she felt a wave of understanding.

"How much did you tell him?" she wondered, letting her hands fall to her sides.

"Very little, actually—that I was in love with another woman, while at the same time in love with my wife, and that I felt I had hastened her death by my other love. Perhaps he half-understood . . . I didn't give him your name, if that worries you."

"Cliff Mason was in college the same year I was a senior," she said irrelevantly.

"And then, moved, I think, by what I had told him. Cliff told me something, *his* confession I suppose you would call it, one he had to make just as deeply as I had to make mine, though what he confessed seemed so lacking in real seriousness as compared with mine. Yet what he said was disturbing, and more disturbing to me today than when he told it to me.

"This morning when they were harping away at Mrs. B.'s on what anybody could write about Cliff in a *memorial* —God what a word!—I kept thinking that his secret confided to me was the only thing about him worth telling, and the one thing, of course, you couldn't write down or that his aunt would ever understand enough to be able to write down."

Huddled up against the largest of the encyclopedias, Rosa Mannheim, despite the season, the heat, the humidity, looked like a woman shrouded in a heavy overcoat, muffler and ear-tabs.

"Mrs. Barrington's harping on what anybody might know about Cliff finally flustered me as much as being there on trial in her house. And she saw what was flustering me, I think. She knew, I'm sure, that I knew something about Cliff. That old woman knows, in a dim way, everything about people, I believe. Her gaze is at times annihilating. Her knowledge hasn't made her any kinder, of course."

"And what did Mrs. Barrington know you knew about Cliff?" Rosa Mannheim asked, her sarcasm and bitterness faintly dissipated.

He puffed on his pipe, not looking at his wife.

" 'Professor Mannheim,' I can still hear Cliff's voice, '*I think I've taken some money that doesn't belong to me while I was under the influence the other night. At the going-away party Willard Baker gave for me . . .*' "

"He had stolen some money?" she asked with indifference.

"He had four thousand dollars on his person he could not account for. He offered to go get the money to show me, but I told him I was sure he hadn't taken it voluntarily.

"His uncle had been away overnight on one of his real-estate deals, as often happened, and the boy was alone. Since he was to be inducted into the army in two days, Willard Baker, on the spur of the moment, thought it would be fun to give the boy a going-away party that night, his pre-induction shindig . . . Cliff went, and for the first time in his life got pie-eyed. He was still in bed drunk, with his clothes on, when his uncle returned the next afternoon from his deal. Even Boyd finally realized what had happened, for the boy's clothes stank of alcohol and where he'd been sick. Then when the old man tried to help him into clean pajamas, the four thousand dollars fell out of his coat pocket. Both the uncle and Cliff were terrified . . .

"They decided—the uncle was sure the boy was innocent —that they had best do nothing and wait until somebody asked for the money back. I think Boyd finally put the money in a strong box, with a note of explanation inside. I never heard a word about it after that. I've tried, in fact, to forget it. I think until yesterday I had. Then at Mrs. Barrington's the whole thing came back in vivid relief, until I felt I had had a hand in it, and in the end the whole thing would be discovered."

"Everybody in town knows that Williard Baker and Vernon Miller are homosexuals," Rosa said, with the certainty that this statement explained everything. "And I imagine Cliff must have known it too, living next to them, and he probably was aware of how he came by the money."

"I don't think Cliff knew anything," Professor Mannheim said, and his voice contained tones of deep disappointment and anger.

"Frankly I don't care," she resumed her old manner. "I don't care about Cliff Mason, or whether he got money wrongly or accidentally, and I don't care whether he's dead or alive . . . And I suggest you forget about it, too. You've got five years to retirement. Shut up and keep indoors, to yourself, is my advice to you. Give old Alma Mason his exam papers, if you have to, and wash your hands of this affair. Otherwise, as somebody who was born and bred in this town, I can warn you: there could be the equivalent of a lynching here with you as the ideal object."

"Thanks, Rosa," he said, but it was clear he had regained some of his strength and dignity.

Sensing this sudden manifestation of change she got up and walked over to him and was about to say something which had every indication of being conciliatory.

"If you don't mind," he cut her short, "would you please leave me alone for now?" He did not look at her. "I have an article to finish," he said in a thick voice.

Her mouth moved to say something but nothing came out, and letting her arms fall from their position of entreaty before her breast, she walked out of the study.

MORE LITTLE TASKS

11

A WEEK after Boyd's and Alma's talks with the old monarch, Ed Shaeffer brought Alma, one morning bright and early, a tiny scented envelope marked *Miss Mason,* which an apologetic, almost unctuous not from Mrs. B. explained that she had been called away again to Washington, but that she hoped everything had been set in motion for Alma to complete her book and that if further help were needed she must write her at Washington.

While still perusing the note, in the library, Alma heard the motor of Mrs. B.'s Cadillac, and looking out the window, spied the old monarch departing for the railway station.

Going back to her desk, Alma put down the note of of delicate lavender paper, and as she did so, her hand touched the "Record" book. She opened it languidly. Only a few indecisive "sentence fragments" looked up at her.

Gently, but almost finally, she lifted the book from the desk and put it away in a drawer stuffed with tissue paper. She closed the drawer.

As she did so, she felt a sudden loosening of tension.

Since their interviews with Mrs. B., she and Boyd had done nothing but argue and debate, and in the heat of wrangling, she had come finally to the chilling and uneasy suspicion that in planning the memorial she had set out to do something which was not only the height of folly, but had made everyone else in the neighborhood behave like fools. Her face and breast covered with crimson as she thought of what had occurred. At the same time she felt that all her neighbors—Mrs. B., Faye Laird, Clara Himbaugh, Mrs. Van Tassel, not to mention Professor Mannheim and Boyd, *expected* her to write something, even if only a page and Cliff's biography was, one might say, publicly commissioned.

Mrs. Barrington's sudden exodus to Washington therefore gave Alma a kind of respite and breathing spell, and she was determined to devote herself only to pleasant tasks around the yard, the kitchen, and the gift shop.

Alma was always secretly glad when the old monarch was gone, and she expected the other neighbors felt likewise.

She could walk about her yard now, doing such improvements as she saw fit—removing dead leaves from the myrtle bed, trimming the hedge, inspecting the tulip trees and the snow-ball bush without feeling that Mrs. B.'s eyes were resting on her with pity and condescending sympathy, and with total freedom of envy.

As she worked this morning about the myrtle bed, she could not help being aware of Willard Baker sitting on his front porch rocker, his Havana shirt open over his chest and stomach, exposing a rug of bright red hair beginning to gray.

Half consciously Alma was glad he sat there, for thinking about Willard, disturbing as it might be, was some relief from thinking about the memorial or Professor Mannheim, and she could think of Willard's shortcomings without having to go on worrying about her own.

Willard fanned himself luxuriantly with a palm-leaf fan, his shirt moving rhythmically in his own propelled breeze. Only his toupee, so life-like indoors, now dead under the movement of the fan, did not yield.

Putting down his fan, he lit a fresh cigar. Then partially buttoning his shirt, he sauntered down the steps in his sandals, and called a greeting to Alma.

She looked up from her work, and greeted him in return, with more affability than either of them could ever remember.

"Another scorcher of a day," he told her.

She nodded, then said after a moment, "It's a bit cooler on the grass."

"Except for air," he complained. "There is no air."

She nodded again.

"Did you see Mrs. B. go off on another junket this A.M.?" he asked. "I suppose it was Washington again," he giggled.

"It was Washington," Alma corroborated his remark a bit gravely.

"I hope I will be able to gad as much as that when *I* am ninety," Willard laughed.

"She's a remarkable old lady." Alma began to withdraw now, as Willard stood immediately beside her.

"Of course, all her life, everything has been done for her, being an heiress you know. And all that money and all those servants . . ." He looked down at the cutting instrument for weeds which Alma held in her hand. "I guess everything she has ever done she has done as play. And as soon as one thing no longer interests her, she drops it, and goes on to something else."

Alma considered this.

"She's self-sufficient, it's true," Alma tried to give his remark her acceptance.

"Exactly!" Willard showed his pleasure she had agreed. "I don't think she has ever needed *anybody*. Certainly she never needed her husband."

Willard waited, perhaps for the effect of his remark to take on Alma. When she was noncommittal, he went on:

"Of course she dotes on her grandchildren and her great-grandchildren. But they're just part of her thousands of other interests. Her life is gadding, I'd say. People give her her excuse to gad."

Alma laughed in spite of the fact Willard had said this.

"You know," he went on, warming up, "her husband had wanted to be a painter instead of a corporation lawyer. At least so he told his friends. She made him see he was a lawyer. You know he used to complain that he hardly ever knew where she was, while she always, of course, knew where he was—in the corporation law office."

"We've almost all forgotten there was a Mr. Barrington," Alma remarked, entering partially into the spirit of his talk.

"I think the old girl has, too," Willard winked maliciously.

"Alma stepped back a pace, then, head up, she said: "I suppose you'll be off to Michigan before too awfully long, yourself." She made reference to his annual summer vacation.

"Oh, Vernon and I are packing now, as a matter of fact. At least he is," and Willard jerked his head back in the direction of his upstairs. "We should be gone by tomorrow. I sometimes wonder though, Alma, if there is a cool place in the whole United States any more, once summer really comes."

"The main thing I suppose is to keep occupied," Alma said almost inaudibly.

"Speaking of keeping occupied," he began, and then stopped to cough his violent cough. "When are you and Boyd taking a vacation?"

"Oh, we don't work hard enough to need one," she joked.

They both laughed somewhat stentoriously.

The door to Mrs. Van Tassel's opened, and Minnie Clyde Hawke came down the walk, her face covered generously this morning with a white powder, and her mouth unevenly outlined with crimson lipstick. She carried her cane loosely today, like an umbrella, and she did not look in their direction.

They could hardly help staring at her.

"Minnie," Willard nodded to Alma significantly.

Alma scraped off some soil from the weeder, and let it fall to the myrtle bed. She pushed the weeder toward her in a nervous gesture then suddenly cautious of its sharp end, brought it away from her body.

"I wonder, Alma, if I could ask you a big favor?" He lowered his voice, and touched her bare arm gently.

Her surprise kept her from replying.

"Don't do it, of course, if you don't want to. But I always think of you and Boyd as the last of the real people around here . . ."

"I'd be glad to do you a favor if I can," Alma responded to his appeal to the old neighborhood, the old times, but her manner was dubious.

"Well, it's really nothing mysterious or to be afraid of. It's my mail. I don't like to ask Clara Himbaugh to do it every year, you know. I'll feel less obligated to her if I don't. You know, Alma, I half-went into Christian Science, I think, just to pay her back for taking care of my mail. But I'd like to back out now."

Alma laughed.

"I'd be delighted to forward your mail," she cried, fired with enthusiasm at the thought of stepping in between Clara and a proselyte. "I had no idea she was working on you, too, Willard."

"I'm afraid I'm an easy mark," Willard laughed, and he looked off momentarily in the direction of his house.

"She's after Faye, too," Alma volunteered.

"She may get *her*," Willard winked.

"I'm afraid you're right."

"Well, we can't stop people from joining the wrong church, eh, Alma?" Willard laughed and this time she smelled the liquor on his breath.

She managed to smile, agreeing.

"I don't think she'll have much of a chance with you, though," Willard went on. "Or Mrs. Barrington either. You two strong-willed ladies."

Touching Alma's arm briefly, Willard said, "If you'll wait just a minute, I'll bring you the keys to the house and the mailbox."

Alma nodded.

He was back in a moment with some keys, which seemed, owing to their shining so in the sun, to have been only recently duplicated.

He handed her a piece of paper on which he had written his Michigan address.

"And if you get tired of sitting home with Boyd," Willard told her, "come over to our place, walk around, stretch your legs, turn on the TV set, anything you like. The liquor cabinet is left open, too, Alma." He winked, knowing her stand on alcohol.

Stopping suddenly and putting his feet together in a kind of military stance, he forced out the words:

"Vernon is sure Cliff will be back, Alma."

Seeing her impassive at the unexpected shift of subject, and the unexpected mention of Vernon, he added almost inaudibly, "Cliff and Vernon were near the same age, and somewhat friendly."

"I hope he's right," she said absentmindedly.

"Of course he's right. Vernon's nearly always right about everything, though nobody believes that but me."

"It's always good to have a friend," Alma turned slightly away from him, "That you can rely on."

"I guess Vernon is my Christian Science maybe." Willard could laugh again.

He coughed suddenly with such violence that Alma was about to ask him if she could bring him something.

"All this," Willard explained his cough, "is what Mother used to call summer complaint." He wiped his mouth with a handkerchief, turning his head away.

"Combined in any case, Alma," he turned about again, "with galloping old age."

"Don't let's get started on that now," Alma joked, but there was concern and gentleness in her voice.

"Alma, you look younger than you did five years ago," Willard told her. Her almost childish expression of pleasure was her thank-you.

"You're certain forwarding my mail isn't a hardship on you?"

"It's what I need," she said. "More little tasks, Willard," and she thought now, almost with panic, of the unfinished memorial.

"Goodbye, Alma." He extended his hands to hers.

"Have a good rest, Willard," she said, and as she looked at him, she could remember again, as if present before her eyes, the faces of his brother Doctor Joe, old Dr. Baker, and Mrs. Baker as they had all looked sitting on the front porch of a summer day. From her mind's picture she looked back again at Willard briefly—his toupee, the deep lines of his face, his open Cuban shirt. Time, she thought, was so odd: things changed imperceptibly for a while, then unrecognizably.

Two days after Willard Baker's conversation with Alma in the yard, he and Vernon Miller rode off together in their station wagon en route to Michigan. Willard who no longer drove, waved to everybody they saw on Peninsula Drive, and indulged in his customary witticism that Rainbow would now be a lot cleaner place without him, and the mayor could start taking in the sidewalks again at dusk.

Alma had heard the station wagon drive off, but she did not look up from the dish pan, absentmindedly keeping her hands in the hot suds until the cry of the noon-day factory whistles brought her out of her day-dreaming.

Her eyes caught a reflection of the keys Willard had given her, hung on a nail near the stove, where their fresh metallic surface caught every reflection, and sometimes, when she entered the kitchen hurriedly, temporarily surprised, almost blinded her, with their flashing scintillation.

The jays screamed in the yard now, it seemed, almost constantly, and with the heat came the odor of burning ketchup, increasing in pungency and strength.

"I had no idea Cliff had a friend in that Vernon Miller," Alma told Boyd as they sat down to supper the evening of Willard's departure.

Boyd had only grunted when Alma told him she had agreed to be custodian of Willard's mail.

But when she mentioned Vernon, he pretended deafness.

She repeated her statement, and Boyd made his accustomed gesture of passing his hand quickly by his ear, meaning he had not heard and she need not bother to repeat.

"I think it is high time you were fitted for a hearing aid," she roared at him.

"You don't need one in the least, of course," he shouted back.

"I can at least hear a thing when it's been repeated twice!"

"I want to be deaf where some things are concerned!"

Tonight it was she who finished her supper first, while Boyd excused his lack of appetite on the heat and the confounded smell of ketchup.

"We look forward all year to summer," Alma said, "and when it comes, we pay attention only to the annoyances."

"Damned company ought to make their product a mile or so under the earth," he grumbled, putting his napkin in the ring and excusing himself.

With the coming of late summer and the departure of Mrs. B. and Willard, a lethargy came over Alma concerning nearly everything but her tasks in the kitchen and yard, and her forwarding of Willard's mail.

She purposely pushed Cliff and the memorial to the bottom of her thoughts in a kind of extraordinary gesture of self-protection. She would wait for fall, she told herself, and cool evenings.

The bulk and number of letters which Willard and Vernon Miller received astonished her. She had forgotten, if she ever knew, that private persons engaged in such voluminous correspondence. The amount of foreign mail was especially surprising: Morocco, Spain, Japan, India, and less surprising, France and Germany.

She attempted to interest Boyd in the foreign postmarks, but he either did not hear or again pretended not to.

At the end of the first two weeks, nearly fifty letters had arrived for the two men. She personally took the mail directly to the postoffice for forwarding.

Finding herself with so many free hours, and feeling at loose ends, Alma took it upon herself to do a little housework for Willard.

The first week she cleaned the downstairs, watered his plants, and tidied up the kitchen, which needed a thorough going-over.

The next week she began on the upstairs.

The largest and most beautiful of the sleeping rooms, however, the one which had been old Mrs. Baker's, in fact, she found unaccountably locked, and as she tried the knob, she saw that the door had been double-locked, and a chain placed against it from inside. Even under the stoutest pressure, the door refused to budge.

Alma supposed he kept some valuables there, and she could not help being critical of his leaving them, if they were there, even behind locked doors.

Coming out of the front door of the Baker house, Alma ran directly into Clara Himbaugh. They greeted one another almost effusively, and Alma was relieved to see that Clara had no feeling of resentment at all in not having been asked to take care of Willard's mail. Besides Clara put Alma's mind to rest; she was going to spend the rest of the summer in Boston for some intensive study and training at the Mother Church.

Clara was about to move on, when Alma, blushing slightly at her own feelings of curiosity, asked:

"Do you by any chance know why Mother Baker's old room is locked up so tight?"

Clara stopped short, perhaps surprised by Alma's seeming nosiness. Alma could see that she hesitated a good while before replying.

"That's Vernon's room," she said finally. "I think he has some valuable things in there from foreign countries."

"Vernon has old Mrs. Baker's room?" Alma could not help commenting.

"Willard didn't want it," Clara said drily.

"I'm sorry I have never got to really know young Vernon," Alma said somewhat abashed.

"He's had a lot to overcome," Clara remarked, and Alma felt that Clara had not been idle in his case either.

"Did he know . . . Cliff?" Alma spoke with casual indifference.

"They saw a bit of one another, I think," Clara replied with more certainty on this subject than on many. "But not too much," she was firm now.

"What a beautiful old house it still is," Alma sighed looking back at it, as the two women walked off now together.

"They built things so well in those days," Alma continued her train of thought. "All that wonderful oak downstairs, the fireplaces, the marble, and all."

Clara nodded, but one could see that her mind was not on houses or material, and Alma supposed she was already thinking of her visit to Boston.

12

In his bed, facing Willard Baker's house now illuminated from within by the feeble glow of a burglar lamp, Boyd resigned himself to a night of unabated insomnia. The depressing flicker of the distant lamp brought back to him half-forgotten visions of the Baker family and the final pitiful tragedy which had spared only Willard who, by reason of his character and antics, seemed to bear no connection with the Baker name or house, so that he resembled a squatter rather than an heritor.

Boyd blamed his sleeplessness on the fact that he was angry Alma had entangled herself with Willard even to the slight extent of being caretaker for his—and of all people, Vernon Miller's—mail. He distrusted and feared these two men to the extent of wishing something would happen to prevent their return from Michigan. Then, ashamed and even shocked by such a wish, he muttered a kind of half-prayer for forgiveness to whatever powers might control the universe.

The court house clock struck one.

Unexpectedly a thought came now to him which he had for a long time forcibly put from his mind—the mystery of the four thousand dollars entrusted to him before his departure by Cliff.

He knew dimly but with almost savage sureness that in some way this money must be connected with the blight of Willard Baker's existence, and yet, having always closed his eyes to such things, Boyd was unable to find any clue or reason for the money being in Cliff's hands. The whole affair seemed both meaningless and significant. He knew, nonetheless, as certainly as ever that his nephew was innocent of any wrongdoing.

At the same time, the four thousand dollars were his strongest link to Cliff. It was the only secret they had ever shared, the only moment, actually, they had been close to one another when, removing his nephew's jacket, stinking with vomit, he had picked up the bills before the boy's incredulous eyes. Cliff could never have confided in his aunt at such a moment, that is, he could never have convinced her of his innocence, and Boyd had jealously guarded this secret as his one proof Cliff had cared more for him than for her.

Then perhaps for the first time, clearly and in words repeated over and over again in the black illumination of insomnia, Boyd told himself that he would have liked—he would have given anything—for Cliff to be his son. He could admit this now. His long and voracious hunger for a son—which the pedestrian routine of his life had deadened but not appeased—suddenly asserted itself with a clarity like an explosion in space.

An agonizing pain in his chest made him get out of bed.

He paced in his bare feet being careful to walk lightly even in his pain lest he rouse Alma and have to go through the weary business of explaining to her his being awake.

Then, with the sudden impulse of instinct, he went to the strong box. The four thousand dollars were still there. He pressed the bills tightly in his finger tips, then put them back for safekeeping. In some oblique way, the money being there after all this time signified that Cliff himself still lived—though all these months he had struggled to keep from Alma the manifestation of his own strong unbelief.

The unexpected clarity of his feelings toward Cliff gave some relief to him now from pain, and sent him back to his attempt at sleep.

Sinking into unconsciousness he felt, for the first time since they had received the telegram informing them the nephew was "missing," the certainty he would really be back. What else, he thought, did he have to live for but Cliff's return?

Dreaming, Boyd saw a hydrogen bomb fall on Rainbow Center.

A flash of something did seem an actuality, from across the way, as he sat up in bed. Then letting his eyes settle on one point in the dark, he could have no doubt. Willard Baker's house—apparently a room upstairs—was on fire. The sputtering burglar light was extinguished in the general illumination of the blaze.

He pulled on his trousers over his nightgown.

Hurrying toward the staircase, he fell heavily against a chest of drawers in the hall, and the blow sent hurtling down the steps an old water pitcher dating from the era before indoor plumbing.

Alma was up and out of bed, almost at once, dressed in a kimono of her mother's.

"What in God's name are you up for," she cried.

"The Baker house is on fire," he spoke through his heavy breathing, for his chest had begun to pain him again.

"Do you know where the keys to the house are?" she watched him narrowly.

He stopped, like one trying to remember where he is.

"The keys are hanging in the kitchen," she informed him. "Do you hear me?"

He nodded.

"I'll call the fire department while you open up the house." She continued to watch him with uneasiness, as he walked away from her.

A few minutes later, opening up the Baker house, Boyd felt some relief when he saw that the blaze was not yet completely out of control, and still confined largely to the one upper room.

He hurried up the stairs, panting and gasping for breath.

The conflagration was in the large bedroom which had once been Mrs. Baker's. He tried the door, but it was secured with the precaution one would bestow on a bank vault.

"God damn fool of a Willard," he muttered.

"Don't try to open that door," he heard Alma's voice now behind him. "I might have known it would be that one," she went on. "It's double locked, bolted, heavens knows what else. I'll fetch something to break it down. . . ."

She disappeared below.

Boyd swore some more to himself, leaning against the wall for support.

"Did you call the fire department?" he wondered, hearing her ascending steps. Catching sight of her, he stared in surprise. She was armed with an axe.

"You're a picture," he laughed weakly.

He offered to take the axe from her, but she motioned him back.

"Don't overexert yourself." She scrutinized his face, then looked away.

Alma struck at the door with slow awkward and decisive blows, while Boyd, stepping far back, shook his head dubiously.

In impatience, she suddenly hit the door above the lock, striking there with growing vehemence.

With a spine-tingling screech, the door gave, and opened under the last fury of Alma's blow.

Inside the bedroom, flames were shooting up from a wastepaper basket, which had, in turn, ignited with some drapes. The fire had nearly consumed the drapes and was now licking against the pale blue wallpaper.

The room bore evidence of being used as a kind of artist's studio. There was an easel, paints, anatomical models, some reproductions of Renaissance statues. But their eyes came to rest on something suddenly brought into arresting life by the flames, and which for the moment deprived them of speech.

An almost life-sized series of photos of the nephew, stretched across the walls of the room by wires, raced giddily before them in the reflection and consummation of the fire. Why they had not seen the photographs at once, they did not know. Together with the flames and the hour of the night, Cliff seemed, burning in the conflagration of the room, about to speak, his one hand extended to them, as if in life, in an eloquent orator's gesture.

It was a groan from Boyd that brought Alma back to herself.

He lay doubled up with pain on the floor.

"What is it, Boyd, for God's sake?" she said, leaning over him.

From below came the nightmarish scream of the fire engines and a vague sound of awakening unrest from the town.

Two firemen had entered the room as Alma kneeled over her brother.

"Could one of you help me?" she said, rising, when they approached her. "I think it's his heart."

Alma turned, then, feeling someone pressing her shoulder, and looked into the white strained face of Faye Laird.

Boyd's convalescence from the heart attack was a slow, but on the whole, an agreeable one for both him and Alma.

Ensconced in a large room downstairs converted from a storage place, he could give himself over at last to slow small tasks which had needed doing for a long time, while enjoying the feeling of giving up for the first time in his life.

Alma was pleased, too, with having to wait on Boyd hand and foot, for at last she had a task commensurate with her energy and time, and her usual irritability and fussiness disappeared in her role as nurse.

A mild attack of angina pectoris was the medical diagnosis, and the doctor had added that Boyd, with proper care, would soon be up and doing and better than new again.

The fire at Willard Baker's had turned out to be not so serious, though nearly everything inflammable in the room had been damaged or destroyed, including the inexplicable photographs of Cliff, which nobody discussed or mentioned.

Immediately Alma was certain Boyd was going to pull through, she had telegraphed Willard what had occurred, but urged on by Boyd had added to her message that he should under no circumstances interrupt his vacation, and if he would forward instructions, she would take care of everything connected with the fire. It was Vernon Miller who had replied to her telegram with another, informing her that Willard was not feeling up to par and they would, therefore, in any case stay on in Michigan until the first cool weather. Vernon thanked her for her solicitude and sent her, much to her irritation, a check for $25.00, "for her trouble."

One afternoon, about a month after the fire, Faye Laird, Mrs. Van Tassel, and Clara Himbaugh—the latter had delayed her trip to Boston because her duties required her presence closer home—were all at Alma's visiting and, inevitably, enjoying cake and coffee.

They had already discussed Boyd's remarkable recovery, and some few awkward questions had come through about the photographs of Cliff in Vernon Miller's bedroom, when the real news of the neighborhood came to their full attention. This was the conversion of Minnie Clyde Hawke.

Two or three weeks after the fire at Willard Baker's, Mrs. Hawke had gone down to the trestle over the river, and in a brief if ostentatious gesture observed only by some Negro children and two or three railroad workmen, had thrown her cane into the dwindling stream below. Then she had extended her arms to the setting sun, and walked resolutely, head erect, back to Mrs. Van Tassel's.

Since that day, Mrs. Hawke had not touched a drop of liquor and, as she told Clara Himbaugh, would no more think of doing so than join a spaceflight to the moon.

Alma had been somewhat taken aback by the conversion, if not disappointed, and added, somewhat drily, "I only hope it's a lasting cure."

"Oh, I'm sure it's all of that," Mrs. Van Tassel raised her voice. "She's no more the person she was than tomorrow is today."

Clara Himbaugh smiled and half-closed her eyes.

"Her whole attitude, her whole appearance has changed," Mrs. Van Tassel continued with her eulogy of Mrs. Hawke, and it was easy to see that Mrs. Van Tassel was unaccustomed to conversions.

Faye Laird and Alma exchanged looks, but Mrs. Hawke's landlady continued:

"It has changed my whole day, too. I used to worry all the time for fear she would set fire to the house. You see she smoked like a chimney, in addition to her drinking, and do you know I don't think she touches cigarettes now either?"

Faye Laird looked away at the mention of tobacco, and sipped from her coffee cup.

110

When all three women now turned to Clara as a kind of tacit compliment to her on her victory in bringing Mrs. Hawke over to a higher life, Clara merely said, "'This is the work of the Great Physician, ladies. I was only the unimportant means of His cure."

"You worked with Minnie Hawke night and day," Alma said, correcting her.

Clara smiled, and reaching over, patted Alma's arm lightly. "You dear person," she said.

"Without Clara, there would have certainly never been this miracle," Mrs. Van Tassel made what appeared to be her final comment.

Alma insisted on cutting them all seconds of her marble sponge cake, while each of the women protested she could not eat another bite, then accepted her helping with grumbling anticipation.

Occasionally, Boyd would call in to them, adding a witticism or joking comment on their gab, to their increased enjoyment.

The ladies discussed Mrs. Laird's health briefly, and agreed summer was hard on the sick and well alike. They complimented Alma on having the good sense to have laid away the book she was writing on her nephew until the cooler weather—although that would soon be upon them before they knew it, and then they all praised the perfectly beautiful weather in Rainbow Center.

Everything suddenly did seem right with the world, and Mrs. Van Tassel, to the mild astonishment of everybody, spoke of having attended a lecture at the Knights of Pythias hall, where, of all people, Professor Mannheim had lectured on the subject, "Can the Young American Intellectual Come of Age?"

Alma was about to say that she did not know Mrs. Van Tassel attended college lectures, when she thought better of it.

Everybody wondered, too, why Mrs. Barrington continued to stay in Washington so long when it was the last place on earth to be in summer time.

"I have heard, from a person whose word I rely on," Mrs. Van Tassel began hesitantly, for she had an aversion to open gossip, "that a certain elder statesman in the capital relies a great deal on Mrs. B.'s friendship—would, in fact, be happy if she decided to settle there."

Cries of pleasure and disbelief followed Mrs. Van Tassel's statement, but all agreed that Mrs. B., marriageable or not, would never submit herself again to the yoke of matrimony.

The ladies had all risen and were giving their goodbyes, their voices rising higher and higher in crescendo, when

Faye drew Alma's attention to the fact that a Western Union delivery boy was standing at the screen door.

"Why on earth didn't he ring the bell," Alma cried, her face still flushed from laughter, and she took the telegram from the boy, and thanked him.

"I expect it's another message from Willard," Alma told the girls. "He's probably not satisfied with the way I've been looking after his affairs," she joked.

"Oh, Willard would *never* criticize you," Clara quipped, entering into the spirit of Alma's remarks.

Alma's gaiety and smiles had frozen on her face to a peculiar look, both stupid and enigmatical—was it overwhelming surprise, or what? None of her friends had ever seen quite this expression on Alma's face, and its singularity hushed them into silence.

Faye moved over to Alma, as if she understood.

"We must not let Boyd know what this telegram says, ladies," Alma addressed them. "Not so much as by a sound." She handed the message to Faye.

All the ladies gathered round Faye Laird.

The telegram, very short, was from the War Department, and informed Miss Alma Mason that the death of her nephew Cliff Mason had been definitely established, and that further information would be forthcoming when available.

While the ladies were studying the telegram, Alma went softly to the door of Boyd's room, looked in, then closed the door.

"Fortunately, he is sleeping," Alma addressed her friends.

"Don't you think you should sit down, dearest," Mrs. Van Tassel inquired, touching Alma's shoulder lightly.

"No, I don't think so," Alma replied in the self-contained slightly hard voice she had employed in the classroom in moments of disciplinary crisis.

"I have to think now of Boyd," Alma explained. "I can't afford not to be strong for him. During his illness," she struggled with the effort to tell this particular thing, "when he was perhaps a bit beside himself, he called and called for his nephew. I had not realized until then how much Cliff had come to mean for him, you see. He was all the son Boyd felt he had. . . . I think I realized then that it was Boyd who cared for him perhaps the most, while you see it was I who always talked and talked . . . and was going to write the book."

The ladies, standing like members of a church choir who have just finished singing an anthem, said nothing, silenced as much by the sudden evidence of Alma's strength as by the annihilating message of the telegram. Whatever was weak or querulous or unsure in Alma had gone, and only her strength was left.

"I had hoped against hope was all," Alma said. "But what I had hoped was not to be."

Faye Laird handed back the telegram to Alma, and Alma took it and folded it gently.

"Yet in a way, ladies," Alma went on in her strong clear voice, "I am glad it is over, and Cliff, too, can come home now in one way or another. We will know now where he is."

As if to make up for Alma, who would not cry, the short controlled weeping of Mrs. Van Tassel broke the silence which had come after Alma's speech, and then came the sudden broken sobs of Faye, and the quiet tears of Clara Himbaugh.

After they had recovered a bit, they each kissed Alma and promising to return that evening, left her, one by one, for they could see she wished now to be alone with her news.

A PROPOSAL OF MARRIAGE

13

LATE one evening a week later, after giving Boyd his medicine and a sedative, and kissing him noiselessly on his forehead, Alma sat in the adjoining room in Mother's chair and listened to the radio, turned down, because of her brother's condition, to the merest whisper.

Lulled to sleep by the broadcast of a string orchestra, Alma awoke with an abrupt start from her chair under the impression a man had entered the room and told her that Willard Baker and Vernon Miller had been seriously injured in an auto accident.

Then she realized she was hearing an announcement of an accident on the radio. The announcer repeated his story of a serious accident, but she was unable to hear the names of those involved, and a sudden spatter of static drowned out the commentator's voice.

So vivid had been the impression of hearing Willard Baker's and Vernon Miller's names, she attempted frantically to get news programs on other nearby stations, which were one by one going off the air. The local Rainbow station was already silent.

She walked back to the kitchen and looked out at the Baker house. The night light, put on earlier by her own hands, was burning, and one would hardly have known now that there had been a fire. Mrs. Baker's old room had already been partially repaired, and newly wall-papered and would soon be habitable again.

Alma decided that she had doubtlessly imagined hearing Willard's name in her concern over the house, and in the aftermath of Cliff's death.

But she had no desire now to go to bed. She sat on in her chair, with the radio playing mutely. At times she dozed off into intermittent unrestful sleep.

The sound of a car's motor awakened her. Listening she heard footsteps coming up the walk to her door. Their precise sound told her the lateness of the hour.

Disturbed, she got up and stood before the door. She turned on the porch light and stared out through the curtains. Then she recognized Faye Laird.

"What on earth are you doing out?" Alma muttered, opening the door for her friend.

114

"Do you mind terribly my coming in?" Faye inquired.

When Alma, distracted by the haggard appearance of the younger woman, did not reply at once, Faye went on: "I saw your light or I would never have disturbed you."

"Something has happened," Alma replied.

"I shouldn't have come," Faye half-muttered to herself.

"Why do you say that?" Alma had recovered her composure now. "We can't carry our burdens alone," she added, but she had turned very pale as she said this.

"Sit down over here, Faye." She motioned to the chair she had occupied a few minutes before.

Without moving, Faye said, "It's Willard Baker and Vernon Miller."

"I know, Faye," Alma told her, more to quiet the rising crescendo of Faye's emotion than to prevent her from speaking.

"Willard is dead, and Vernon may not pull through," Faye said, then, as if to inform herself.

"Faye," Alma whispered. "I didn't know—I only guessed. Please tell me what happened."

Faye showed no surprise at Alma's sudden reversal of her statement.

"I just came back from the hospital at Mt. Pleasant," the younger woman explained. "They telegraphed me this afternoon—I went over there without telling anybody here. It was a head-on collision with a truck, a drunken driver, I believe. It was not Vernon's fault . . . Willard died instantly . . . They had decided to return on the spur of the moment. Vernon was worried about the fire and about things being destroyed in his room."

"I was going to have the room all fixed up for them," Alma said, "so they would hardly have known anything happened."

Faye nodded.

"I cant take it quite all in," Alma remarked.

"I should have waited until morning to tell you," Faye returned to her apology. "But there was nobody else to tell."

"I don't know why you keep saying that," Alma said with a flash of temper. "This is the place you should have come, and I am the person you should have spoken to. Who else is there?"

"You have so much composure, Alma."

"No," Alma replied. "I'm afraid to let go is all."

"I had my cry out on the way here," Faye explained.

Alma shaded her eyes with her hand, but not because she was weeping.

"Alma," Faye's voice came now steady and willful. "I

must tell you something else. Perhaps it's because of it that I had to see you tonight, who knows."

"Go on," Alma said, with weary strength.

"In the hospital," Faye struggled with what she would say, "in that ward where they took me in to see Vernon . . ."

Alma waited for her.

"He asked me to marry him," Faye brought out, and she gave her friend a look of astonished supplication.

"Vernon Miller asked you?" Alma took her hand away from shading her eyes.

Faye nodded.

"I see," Alma said, her astonishment nullified by that of Faye's.

After a pause, Alma said, "What did you say to him?"

"What was there to say? I said I would."

Alma stared at her, openly blank.

"What would you have said?" Faye demanded.

Alma rose and walked stealthily up and down the room. After a minute or more, her back to Faye, she asked, "Do you love him?"

"I don't know," Alma heard the reply.

"I never knew you and this man ever saw one another," Alma raised her voice slightly. "No one ever saw you together at any rate."

"We hardly ever did see one another," Faye spoke to Alma's back as one would speak through a confessional.

"Why, I don't know what to tell you," Alma said in an insipid voice which sounded almost gay and silly.

"I felt, Alma, the decision had been made for me somehow even as he asked me in that ward. When he asked me there from all those casts and bandages and that smell of—what is it—ether and disinfectant—I felt I had no personal choice."

"Oh stop it!" Alma cried, but the expression of her voice said *Go on*.

"I felt I had no right to say no," Faye continued. "As he said, he needed me, he *needed* . . ."

"Yes," Alma said, her head held toward her breast.

"You don't think I should marry him, then," Faye cried.

Turning around, her face red and terrible, and prepared for anything else that might be said tonight, Alma answered:

"Did I tell you you should not?"

"Of course you didn't." Faye did not take her eyes away from Alma's face.

Letting her arms fall at her side, and the color draining from her face, Alma said, "It's all so surprising and puzzling, and everything. And then what value would an old maid's opinion have, after all."

116

"A good deal, if the old maid is you, Alma, especially when the other old maid is me."

"Yes," Alma said quietly. "I guess I see."

"If it's his reputation you're thinking about, I'm not afraid of that, if I ever was."

Alma gazed at her.

"You know what I'm talking about, of course." Faye's voice was suddenly sharp and metallic, almost belligerently loud, so that Alma raised her finger to her mouth to warn of Boyd's being asleep in the next room, but Faye mistook this gesture for Alma's reluctance to discuss the subject Faye had brought up.

"You know, of course, everybody has always said Willard and Vernon were homosexuals," Faye said in ringing tones.

"I'm afraid I didn't," Alma said.

Faye stared at her for a good minute and then she saw indeed that Alma did not know.

"You weren't aware of their reputation," Faye said weakly.

"No, Faye, I was not," Alma said, an insipid smile playing about her mouth. "I don't know homosexuals," she added.

"I'm sorry then I told you."

"Don't be sorry about telling me anything," Alma came back at her. "I'm afraid I don't know a good many things."

Then in an almost childish, supplicating voice, Alma said:

"Those reports about Willard and Vernon weren't . . . true."

When Faye did not reply, Alma cried:

"Those reports, Faye, were not true!"

"I don't know," Faye replied. "And I don't care."

"You don't care," Alma repeated, and she turned away again.

"When he asked me to marry him, I felt the decision to say yes had been given to me. It was not my decision, but it was something I felt I had to do."

"It's your life, Faye, and you must do what you feel you should."

Faye walked slowly over to the other end of the room, where Alma had gone, her back to her. She took hold of Alma's arm, gently.

"Forgive me for coming here tonight and upsetting you so."

"There's nothing to forgive, dear," Alma said, still keeping her back to her. Then turning, she looked into Faye's eyes carefully.

"You will come to the right decision in time," Alma said at last. She kissed Faye on the forehead.

"And while we talk like this," Alma said, "poor Willard is dead."

They both gave in to their grief.

"He and his whole family are gone now," Alma whispered as a kind of final valedictory.

Then studying Faye's expression carefully, Alma said:

"The night of the fire, we found a lot of photographs of Cliff in Vernon Miller's room. It was very disturbing to Boyd. What do you suppose they were doing there?"

Faye did not reply at once. "I had heard about the photographs," she said finally. "All I can say is that Vernon was a very good photographer and he liked to photograph anybody he knew."

"Did he take any photos of you?" Alma scrutinized her.

Faye shook her head. "I've really only known Vernon for the past month," she explained.

"And Vernon kept all these photos of Cliff in his room," Alma said, perhaps for her own benefit of understanding.

"I'm sure Vernon never harmed Cliff," Faye said, an edge in her voice.

Alma waited for a moment and then, as if surrendering her doubts and fears, perhaps her understanding, said:

"There's so much we can never know about everything and everybody."

Faye took Alma's hand in hers, and pressed it heavily.

"Good night, Alma, dear, and forgive me."

Then she asked briefly about her brother.

"Boyd is coming round," Alma told her, as if brushing all of the past away but him and his recovery. "The doctor is so pleased with his progress. I haven't told him, though, about Cliff. That's for some time in the future yet. I couldn't let anything happen to Boyd now, you know," she said.

Faye pressed her hand again.

"THE MEMORIAL IS FINISHED"

14

OVER a month later Boyd Mason had recovered sufficiently to pay a brief morning visit to his real-estate office. That afternoon he sat under the grape arbor in the back yard, a thing he seldom did in the days of Willard Baker.

Another convalescent was now within easy view of Boyd. Vernon Miller, laden down with cast and bandages, sat on the Baker porch. Perhaps the young man's encumberances and the fresh memory of Willard's death made his presence seen innocuous to Boyd, for the old man continued to sit on facing his neighbor, and once even nodded to him. Perhaps Boyd's acceptance, too, came in part from Faye Laird's intermittent calls on the young man. Alma had told Boyd that Faye and Vernon were engaged to be married, and to her surprise—if not her relief—Boyd had not been angry, though he was surprised, of course.

Everybody in the neighborhood, too, was aware that Willard had left Vernon the bulk of his property and money, which was more than a considerable fortune.

Alma had told Boyd of the death of Willard Baker a day before the funeral services were held. She had not yet, however, told him of Cliff's death, and now that he had gone to his real-estate office, she faced the realization that she must tell him or let him learn it by a sudden, haphazard and devasting remark offered him by a passerby or a client.

Sitting down beside her brother, as the afternoon began to wane, Alma began the conversation.

"Faye could do worse, I suppose." She nodded in the direction of the Baker porch, where Vernon and Faye were conversing.

"At her age she can't be too choosey," Boyd replied, entering reluctantly into the spirit of Alma's remark.

"He could do worse now, too," Alma went on, thinking of Vernon's new wealth and position.

"He already acts like a different fellow since Willard's gone," Boyd commented.

"Well, let's not blame poor Willard for too much," she said.

"You know," Boyd said, as if to agree with Alma's statement, "his parents kind of made him the black sheep by

119

preferring the younger son all the time, Doctor Joe, to Willard. Everything was Joe Joe Joe, nothing was ever old Willard. His own mother, old Mrs. Baker was, I think, aware of that, for she told our Mother a story once which gave it all away. It seems when the boys were just children, Mrs. Baker heard one of them coming into the front door of the house. She called out from the kitchen, 'Is that my precious treasure Joe?' and the sad little answer came from the parlor, 'No, it's just Willard is all.' Mrs. Baker felt terrible, of course, when she heard that, and she tried in her way to make up for it. But it had all gone too far by then, and Joe stayed right where he was from then on, their favorite, and the star . . ."

Alma did not say anything, immersed in thought.

"Beginning tomorrow," Boyd turned brightly to Alma, in his old manner, "I'm going to begin regular office hours."

"You feel you're strong enough?" she wondered.

He nodded. "You'll have to be thinking of finishing that book you were writing on our boy, Cliff, too," he smiled. "Now that cooler weather is coming."

Alma did not say anything.

"Did you hear what I said?" He raised his voice.

She nodded.

His attention had been distracted by a squirrel, which had suddenly and surreptitiously deposited a walnut near the summer house.

"Sure sign of fall," he pointed out to her.

"Did Professor Mannheim turn over to you those papers of Cliff?" Boyd came back to the subject again.

"I've decided not to write anything about Cliff after all, Boyd," she said in loud expressionless tones.

He scowled.

"After all the fuss and bother everybody's been to in town," his old temper flared—to her relief and yet to her inexpressible sadness.

"The memorial is finished," she said, in words perhaps as surprising to herself as to him.

"You've written it?" he cried, a strange pleasure and surprise on his face.

"No," she replied.

As Boyd scolded her then, for "giving up on the job," as he called it, Alma raised her own voice to say, "Did it ever occur to you that you were all babying me, an old maid schoolteacher with nothing to do, writing a book about a young nephew she didn't really know from Adam or probably understand?"

"We none of us had that thought," Boyd said to her, taken aback.

"Boyd, what if I told you that I had come round to your own feeling, the feeling of the neighborhood and the town—that Cliff was maybe not missing—but dead."

"Then I'd say you'd changed one hell of a lot," he told her. "And you'd be feeling something furthermore that I don't think anybody in this town or neighborhood, and especially me, ever thought. Because we all think he's alive and will be coming home some day."

"Boyd," she said in a voice of quiet caution. She did not know what to do. She could hardly, in any case, prolong telling him much longer in view of his return to his office and the town.

"Are you taken ill or something?" he asked, looking at her with real concern, even anguish.

"Boyd, I think you're strong enough now to hear my news. I've wanted to spare you, but I haven't spared myself. I'm tired enough now to say this to you."

"Alma," he soothed her, unsuspecting, "what's your news?"

"Our boy is dead," she told him. "Cliff is dead."

"Are you speaking of your fears?" he asked in a hushed voice.

"No, it's not my fears any more. A few days after you got sick, the war department informed me. It's a fact he is dead. There wasn't even enough left of him to ship home in the casket. There was nothing of our Cliff left."

Violent sobs, long suppressed, of almost inhuman grief broke from her breast, then quickly subsided into the stunned silence of accustomed pain and, as she had so often remarked in herself, old age.

"Alma, easy, easy," Boyd said in strange composure and tenderness.

She daubed at her eyes.

"There should have been something left," she appealed to him. "There should have been something *from* him for us. And I never knew him, Boyd, I only loved him. I never *knew* Cliff."

"Now, Alma," he stretched out his hand. "We none of us, I'm afraid, know anybody or know one another."

She took his hand in hers, which she had hardly done since they were young, ages ago.

"We're all pretty much strangers to one another," he muttered.

"I'm so glad you're strong," she said. "I'm grateful."

Perhaps his strength had come because he had all along known the truth, or because, as she had said, she had needed and was grateful for his being strong.

That evening, long after her accustomed hour of retiring, Alma awoke in her chair out of a sound sleep, thinking she heard someone calling her. The voice chilled her, for it resembled so much her mother's. Then she recognized, after a moment's fright, Boyd's white hair, and his quiet voice attempting to reassure her.

There was no scolding tone in her expression, as she asked him what he wanted. She knew Boyd would never awaken her unless it was necessary. At the same time, she knew that by his calm this was no immediate emergency, but an old source of trouble.

"I couldn't sleep and came out to get something to drink," he explained. "I saw you hadn't turned in."

Alma turned on the stronger light of the lamp behind her.

"What's that you've got in your hand there?" she wondered.

He looked down at his own hands.

"For pity's sake, Boyd, what does it mean?" she cried.

He extended to her the four thousand dollars which had fallen so long before from Cliff's jacket.

Boyd described to her the events and situation of that past time, omitting none of the details.

"You are certain he had been drinking?" She handed back the money to him. The thought of Cliff and drink was a hurdle difficult enough for her to take.

"One spree in a lifetime isn't a bad record," he told her.

She looked at the bills in his hands again, without speaking for a moment.

"I suppose Willard knew all about this," Alma said.

Then she continued: "But I believe Cliff told you the truth."

"About not knowing where the money came from?" he wanted to make sure he had understood her.

She nodded, but he could see the doubt and uncertainty in her expression.

"You knew Willard's and Vernon's reputations." She looked her brother directly in the eye.

"Oh, sure," he said boldly, avoiding her look.

"They were homosexuals," she said, as if death had closed both Willard's and Vernon's careers.

He looked at her in total surprise.

"Who told you that?" he wondered.

"It wasn't you," she reproached him.

"I don't think there is anything to that story," Boyd said. She saw that perhaps he meant this. "Vernon Miller was a boy Willard practically adopted out of the children's home. Besides, he's engaged to get married."

"I think you've worried about this money and their repu-

122

tation, Boyd, more than you let on now. Why didn't you let me worry along with you about it all?"

"Oh, it was all so hazy. I didn't feel I understood it, and therefore why trouble you with it."

"Nobody ever told me the truth. You never even told me the time you knew Mother was going to die until ... until she died."

"I didn't want to trouble you with suspicions—in this case," and he slapped the roll of bills against his one hand.

"That money isn't suspicion," she said. "It's a fact."

"But Cliff knew no more about it or where it came from than we did!" He raised his voice in defense.

"Granted," she agreed. "But you could have shared your worry with me."

"What are you going to do?" he said, and his concern, his fear, his dependence were so naked and complete she could not help smiling.

"Nothing," she replied to his question. "Unless you think —in all honesty—we could mention the money's existence to Vernon Miller. After all, he's the heir."

"We could do that," Boyd agreed.

"I would have thought a business man such as yourself would have invested the money," she remarked.

"It wasn't quite ... clean," he finished, helpless with that last word.

She did not budge. Finally she said, "We'll have to see Vernon. That is," she said, looking at her brother, "I will go talk to him."

"Don't let him upset you," Boyd seemed to plead with her.

"Why would I?" she wondered.

"We both believe in Cliff," he said, his weary eyes looking down at the carpet.

"Of course we both believe in Cliff," she repeated. "He was ours."

"I was afraid maybe his image had got spotted for you," Boyd said, a kind of childishly hopeful smile on his mouth.

"Spotted?" She seemed surprised.

"I was afraid so."

"I don't think it has," she spoke with puzzlement.

He looked at her again before getting up to leave.

"It has upset things a bit, I suppose," she was guarded.

"It will all come back all right," Boyd told her, meaning, she supposed, Cliff's image.

"Boyd," she called to him just before he stepped out of the room.

He looked back fearfully.

"Those photographs of Cliff in Vernon Miller's room," she asked.

He stood waiting.

"What do you suppose they meant," she asked when he gave her no look or word of assistance. "We have almost no photographs of Cliff. I've hunted and hunted so, wanting more. And there, in the room of a stranger, were all those large photos of him, but somehow not as we knew him, or saw him."

Boyd merely waited as an old and faithful retainer will wait for final dismissal.

"I always thought, Boyd, that it was seeing those photos that brought on your heart attack."

He did not appear to have heard her.

"There was nothing wrong with Cliff," he told her, in stern judicial tones. "You must get that out of your head. He couldn't help if he lived next door to the people he did, or that he had no real parents."

"What?" she cried in her angry customary voice.

"Goodnight, Alma," he changed his expression to one of benediction.

She watched him, soothed in spite of herself by something in his look.

"Goodnight," she murmured after him, almost hypnotically submissive.

A PLOT OF FLOWERS AND TREES

15

About the middle of November, in the midst of a spell of Indian summer, an event occurred which at first bore the earmarks of another neighborhood tragedy.

Minnie Clyde Hawke, in sudden despair, had attempted suicide by taking an entire bottle of Mrs. Van Tassel's sleeping pills. She had been rushed to the nearby hospital, where her condition was found to be not critical. Her near brush with death had cleared her mind—the report was brought back—and she had expressed to Mrs. Van Tassel, more shaken perhaps than her boarder, her eager desire to live and begin seriously her "new life."

Alma had heard the siren of the ambulance the day Mrs. Hawke had been taken to the hospital, but she had refused to budge from her kitchen, no matter who it might be or how close to home. Later Boyd had called her from the office with the news, and told her not to worry.

This morning, the second day of warm weather, the sweetish smell of the ketchup was again just perceptible, and Alma plunged her hands, as many times as she could find excuse for, into the suds of the dish-pan. Drying her hands at last on the tea towel, she walked out on the back porch and looked out across the lawn.

To her surprise she saw that Vernon Miller, his left leg still in a cast, but supporting himself on a cane, had wandered into her yard and was inspecting something clinging to the snow-ball bush.

He smiled at her, and unwilling to turn back, Alma found herself advancing toward him, smiling in return.

"Can you imagine?" she heard his voice. "It's a live butterfly at this time of year." He pointed out to her a white cabbage butterfly, barely alive.

Strange as it might seem, Alma had never before been alone with Vernon Miller. She saw him now as one sees the improbable but the familiar—in a dream.

"It's actually warm today," she referred to the butterfly, and she stepped back in a motion of departing.

"Did you hear the news?" he asked.

Looking at his face carefully, impressed suddenly by its

freshness and openness, she did not reply immediately. She studied his face in gratitude, as it were.

"Miss Mason," he spoke, as if to recall her to attention.

"I heard the ambulance go," she recalled yesterday's event. Then, perhaps concerned by her own appearance of callousness toward Mrs. Hawke, she added:

"It's hard on Mrs. Van Tassel, too."

"Faye has been over there with her today." Vernon looked in the direction of the Van Tassel house. "I expect she's all right now."

"I'll have to go over," Alma said.

Perhaps thinking to herself, Alma said, "Where is Clara Himbaugh?"

The severity of Alma's tone caused Vernon to laugh, and Alma, after a moment of surprise, joined in.

"She's in Boston," Vernon told her still laughing.

Looking toward her own house and then back quickly at her interlocutor, Alma said, "May I invite you inside?"

Vernon did not reply, perhaps because he wished to be consciously slow in his hearing of her invitation.

"I'm baking some bread in the oven, that's why I can't stay on outside," she explained, a bit short now.

"You bake your own bread," he registered his surprise.

"Oh, every so often, when I'm at loose ends," she replied. "Do come in and I'll invite you to a cup of coffee." She started on in.

When he did not follow immediately, she turned back and said: "Watch how you manage the step down there," pointing to an uneven place where the walk dipped precipitously.

"Oh, I walk better now than I did before," he joked.

Inside the kitchen she went through her ceremony, handing him the coffee and a linen napkin.

Then she heard him say, "This is the first time I think I've ever been invited inside a Rainbow house."

She stopped, sorry, in a way, he had said it.

"I've been away teaching for so many years, I haven't yet got the knack of inviting people in as often as I'd like," she told him. "One day, though, I'll feel I'm at home here."

"I didn't mean to say—" he began to explain that he had not meant his remarks as a reference to her.

"I understand what you mean," she said.

"Won't you sit down, too, Miss Mason?" he inquired.

She smiled. "In just a minute I will," she indicated she must still turn her attention to the bread in the oven.

"I'd like you to write something on my cast, too." He pointed out to her a few—a very few—autographs and some attempts at wit on the covering of his leg.

"Of course," she said, not unpleased.

He handed her a pencil, and she laughed, even giggled.

"It's been so long since I wrote anything like this," she explained her hesitation, and she turned a furious red.

"Oh, just write anything," he coached her.

Alma looked a moment at the point of the pencil in the guise of one who catches her cue there. Then bending over his leg, she wrote:

TO VERNON MILLER, FROM HIS FRIEND
AND NEIGHBOR, ALMA MASON

"That's very thoughtful of you," he said, moved, taking back the pencil she proffered him.

"It must be uncomfortable," she motioned to the cast.

He did not reply. Instead, he looked out the window. Then, after a moment, he said, "I'm half-expecting the upholstery man today. He's redone some of the chairs that got soiled in the blaze."

"Oh, the fire," Alma said in the manner of one who had only heard of it.

Then, speaking in her old serious schoolteacher manner, she added, "Mr. Miller, sometime when you are free for a while, I would like to talk with you."

"I'm free nearly anytime," he said, his open frank manner again attracting her notice. "Now if you like," he went on. "That upholstery man may never show up."

"I don't know if now is the right time," she said, looking at the oven.

"Well, I'm always here with this leg," he smiled.

She did not smile or look at him in return.

"It's in a way a rather serious thing," she indicated indirectly what her subject was, and his smile relaxed faintly on his mouth.

"But not alarming, of course," she showed she wanted to spare him, or at least wanted no unpleasantness. "It's a thing, Mr. Miller, which well, now that Cliff is dead—a thing which puzzles his uncle and me."

"Oh," he said, calm.

"I hardly know how to say it, though," she felt her way.

"Well, don't be afraid of hurting my feelings," he helped her, but there was a bit of edge to his voice.

When she did not go on, he colored, and said, "Was it the photographs of Cliff in my room?"

She looked him full in the face, and reassured, or perhaps pleased by what she saw there, she replied, "No, it wasn't the photos, though they were a surprise."

"I was a kind of a photographer in those days," he said, almost inaudibly.

"The thing that worried his uncle and me was a sum of money."

She did not look at him, but she knew her statement had hit home.

"Money," he inquired in a changed voice.

"Four thousand dollars." She looked at him, and the expression on his face satisfied her—she felt she could go on.

"He didn't take it along with him, then," Vernon said, perhaps for himself.

"You gave it to him, Vernon?" She did not look at him now.

"Thanks for calling me Vernon," he said. There was a long pause.

"Oh yes," he replied at last. "It was my money, not Willard's."

"I didn't mean, of course—"

"A wealthy lady who visited me from time to time—Christmases and Easters and those days—at the Children's Home, gave the money to me."

"And you gave it to Cliff?" she wondered.

He nodded.

"But he didn't ask it from you?" She was fearful again.

"Cliff?" Vernon raised his voice, and as he did so she heard in his tone how much Vernon and Cliff must have had in common, however briefly, even if but for a moment, and that she could never have said *Cliff* as he had done just now, with that expression in it of mutuality and common understanding.

"Cliff would have never asked money from anybody, I'm sure," Vernon said. "He was going into the army next day ... I'd had too much to drink. I wanted to give him something. I don't know why—I wanted to help him. As if I could have, or as if the money would have helped."

"You must have thought a great deal of him," she retreated now from the depths she felt she had looked into.

"I loved Cliff," he said.

She kept her gaze fixed on him.

"He was the only person who ever treated me—who, well, who ever *treated* me. He accepted me, the way I am and all."

"I'm glad," she said, and perhaps she was.

He stood up painfully on his cast, and she half-advanced protectively toward him, when he said, "I won't fall, Miss Mason," and waved her back.

"Good heavens!" she cried. "The bread!"

She flung open the oven door, and with cries of disap-

128

pointment and irritation, drew out first two loaves and then a third loaf.

"They're not really burned," she tried to reassure herself. "Just too dark."

She put the loaves on a special wire rack waiting for them on the table, and Vernon followed her over there.

"Miss Mason," he said over her irritation and fluster, "I had to give him the money."

Looking up, she saw without surprise, but with no particular gladness now, that his eyes had tears in them.

"Sit down, Vernon, will you," Alma said at last, patiently kind now. "I want to ask you a favor, perhaps the biggest favor I have ever asked anybody in my life, and I want you to grant it to me."

She waited until he had seated himself beside her.

"You agree?" she wondered.

He nodded.

"Why did you really give Cliff the money?"

"I wish you wouldn't ask that," he told her.

"Why?" she wondered.

"I don't want to hurt you," he said.

"You're sure it's not because you don't want to hurt yourself?"

"No, Miss Mason, I've been hurt all I can be. Don't you think I know what everybody in town has said about me and Willard. I've been hurt all I can . . ."

"You won't want to hurt me," she repeated his excuse. "Well, Vernon, let me tell you something. People have tried *not* to hurt me, to keep things from me all my life. I was one girl in a family of boys. Nobody, my mother, my father, my brothers, none of them ever wanted me to know anything. And in a way I never did. But no matter how often or well they hid the truth from me, it always got to me last, and hurt me then a thousand times more than if they had told it to me at the beginning. Do you understand? Why did you give Cliff the money?"

"I gave him the money because he seemed like myself," Vernon said.

"What does that mean," she wondered, with some asperity.

"Oh not that there was anything wrong with him. He wasn't a homosexual if that's what you're worried about. Cliff hated Rainbow and being here, he wanted to leave home."

"Go on," she urged him.

"Isn't that enough, Miss Mason?" he seemed to warn her. "Don't you know any more, or aren't you brave enough?"

He shook his head sadly, ambiguously.

"Well, be brave enough for once in your life," she raised her voice, and waited.

"Cliff hated Rainbow," Vernon began. "He hated taking your and his uncle's charity. You were his Children's Home. He hated everything, I think. He hated being without parents and thinking he was unwanted. He hated for you to feel you had to love him. He never wanted to come back here or to hear from anybody. He told me, 'If I had the money I would never be back.' 'What if I give you the money, Cliff,' I said to him. He wouldn't look at me and then he began to drink, and when I went and got the money and showed it to him he just stared at it. I told him, 'Cliff, if you hate Rainbow now and all of it, take this, and never come back not even when you're out of the army—do you understand?' But he just drank."

"He just drank," she repeated.

"I had forgot all about it, then, offering him the money, and then when it was very late, almost morning, I was sitting in the front room when he come in the house, and stared at me. I knew he had been drunk, but now he looked more like he couldn't remember what he came in for than anything else. 'Did you change your mind?' I said to him, but he didn't answer. He just stood there staring at me, his hand on the doorknob.

"I went over to where he stood and looked at him. I thought I could see my face and head reflected the way I stood in front of his eyes. When he didn't move, I put the money in his jacket pocket. 'You'll be all right now, Cliff,' I said to him, but he never looked at me after that at all.

"After I gave him the money he turned around and was on his way out to the front door when I thanked him to his back. 'Thanks, Cliff, for taking it,' I said, and he went on out. I knew when I saw him going out why I had given him the money. He was so like me in almost all ways, only I knew he had the courage to go away from here. I never had the courage to run away, from the Children's Home, or Willard, or Rainbow, or myself. I had to stay. I wanted somebody to run off for me, to be free for me. And then that day when I found out that Cliff was dead, after the shock and all, God forgive me, I said, or I prayed maybe, 'Well, Cliff won't never have to come back now, and that was the thing he never wanted to do.' "

Vernon's voice had got lower and lower. How much Alma heard, or half-heard, or never heard, it was hard to tell. She didn't ask him to repeat.

"He couldn't have felt so lost!" Alma said after a while.

Vernon looked at her, but then he saw that she did not believe her own denial.

"Cliff was too proud to admit he needed love from anybody. That, I guess, was his trouble," Vernon told her. "He was too proud to think anyone felt they wanted to love him. He thought nobody could love him or wanted him to stay with them."

"Didn't he know we loved him?" Alma cried.

"No, Miss Mason," Vernon gave her the last of his knowledge. "He only knew he wanted to run off."

They neither spoke for a while.

"Well, Vernon," Alma began at last, "I asked you for the truth, and you told it to me. I may seem grateful or ungrateful. The truth doesn't make you feel thankful, no matter how much you promise you'll give thanks for it."

"No, it don't make you feel thankful, Miss Mason."

"Can't you say *Alma* now?" she asked.

He nodded.

"You told me the truth, and I believe it, but if you think I don't love Cliff all the more for hearing it, you're mistaken. Because I see how much more he needed the little love anyone could give. He was unhappier than we knew."

"Cliff maybe was unhappiness," Vernon said. "Perhaps that was his vocation."

Alma wept quietly, perhaps refreshingly, for she knew it was the last time she would ever really weep for Cliff.

"Alma," Vernon said, standing near her, "if you would use that four thousand dollars as some kind of memorial for him, would you please? Maybe a plot of flowers or flowering trees or something between your property and mine, say?"

"You mean the place where Mrs. Van Tassel wanted to build her greenhouse?"

"We could raise some kind of flowers or trees for him there," Vernon said.

"I'll think about it," she showed her appreciation for the thought.

"Please," he asked now, "as a return for what I've told you, Alma. I couldn't take the money back now."

"I won't give it back," Alma said.

16

ALMA never told Boyd Vernon Miller's story of his putting the money in Cliff's pocket. Indeed now in the old man's weakened state—his memory had begun playing him tricks —she was not certain he would remember anything clearly at all about the painful question of the four thousand dollars. Once when she began—more to relieve her own mind than to inform him—to sound him out about the incident, he had merely looked blank at her. Boyd now lived only in "the specious present."

The sole event of importance of that fall and winter was the wedding of Vernon and Faye, which took place at Christmas time. Mrs. Barrington departed from custom and gave the bride and groom an elegant wedding breakfast, and Mr. and Mrs. Miller departed a few hours later by plane for Portugal.

Just as surprising, perhaps, as such a wedding or such a wedding breakfast, was Faye's letter of resignation to the President of the college and the board of trustees—in which some saw vindication at last for Professor Mannheim. It was a stinging communication which contrasted the college's lofty Christian principles with its dog-eat-dog methods of promotion and dismissal, its pious professions with its heartless practices. Mrs. Barrington, it was said, was given a copy of Faye's letter in the hope the old monarch would express herself on the side of the President and the board. Her answer, apparently, was her wedding breakfast for the betrothed.

Equally unforseen was Faye's decision to leave her mother in the hands of two trained nurses who were total strangers both to the daughter and Mrs. Laird, and whose highest and perhaps only recommendation was their price. Even Alma and Boyd were shocked at this latter decision, but since they had urged Faye over the years to take action nearly this drastic, there was little for them to say when their suggestions became reality.

Mrs. Hawke had taken Mrs. Van Tassel on an all-expenses-paid trip to Charleston, South Carolina, for the Christmas holidays. Clara Himbaugh was again in Boston, so that the entire neighborhood was deserted except for the Masons and Mrs. Barrington who, contrary to custom, and owing to a sudden attack of sciatica, had not gone to Washington for the holidays, and hugged her hearth.

Boyd and Alma, too, hugged their hearth, seldom going out anywhere. Alma's gift shop did a thriving business, and in her spare time from selling pottery and lace, she began experimenting with French and Italian cooking, but at last had to give this up owing to its upsetting effect on Boyd's digestion and because so many recipes called for more wine and brandy than Alma felt was consonant with her own background and position.

The winter that followed was a stern and long one, characterized by strong winds, sleet storms, and heavy snows, and for the first time in the history of the county, gales of an almost hurricane intensity destroyed many stretches of trees and shrubs in Rainbow and vicinity.

Alma, despite her long years of criticism of Mrs. Barrington's passionate cultivation of her acres of flowering trees and shrubs, watched with dismay and finally pity and regret as the recurring storms stripped the old monarch's estate of many of its most beautiful landmarks: the English hawthorn was felled, the horsechestnut blasted, and inevitably the trumpet vine was laid waste.

After an icy spring, Decoration Day arrived damp and chill.

Just at daybreak, in attempting to bring the flag down from the attic, Boyd slipped on one of the narrow upstairs steps, and in trying to break his fall tore the flag rather badly.

Alma said that the important thing was he had not hurt himself, and she was certain she could mend Old Glory and have it up before mid-morning. But the tear was not so easily repaired, she saw, once she began working over it. Other long-hidden snags and rents in the material suddenly asserted themselves, as if in conspiracy with the first rent in the fabric, and soon Alma saw that what she held was a tissue of rotted cloth, impossible to mend. The dry-goods stores were closed, of course, and neither Boyd nor Alma wanted to go to one of the neighbors to borrow a flag.

Alma was about to say that this was the first time in memory that they had not put up a flag on Memorial Day, but the look of concern and disappointment on Boyd's face prevented her from making the remark.

About one o'clock that afternoon, Mrs. Barrington sent Ed Shaeffer over to the house to inquire if everything was all right.

Alma noticed Mrs. B.'s handsome relatively new silk flag

133

fluttering over her front porch as she talked to Ed through the screen door.

"We're both fine, tell Mrs. B.," Alma informed the young chauffeur. "Just tell her we had a little bad luck and tore our flag. That's why it isn't up."

Ed Shaeffer thanked Alma, put on his driver's cap, which he had held ceremoniously in his hand, and with a nod and a wink to let Alma know that the purpose of his call was primarily to satisfy Mrs. B.'s concern over there being no flag this year, he hastened back to inform his employer.

"We'll be getting a new flag, Ed," Alma called after him.

She had only got comfortably into a new game of checkers with Boyd when the doorbell rang again, and she turned to see Ed Shaeffer before the screen door.

"Mrs. B. wonders if it would be ever so much trouble," Ed began his memorized speech, "if you could find the time, Miss Mason, to come over for a few minutes. She's not feeling too chipper, she says to tell you, or she would come pay you a call, and besides she wants to give you something."

"She wants me to come right away?" Alma said, still not having risen from her chair by the checker board.

"To tell you the truth," Ed lowered his voice, "she had a bad spell last night. Don't tell her I told you. The Doc doesn't want her out of bed until at least tomorrow. She overdid fixing up the trellis by the summer house."

"Go over and see her," Boyd said sharply, irritated by Alma's lethargic dilatoriness.

"Tell Mrs. B. I'll be along directly," Alma said to the boy, and she went to fetch her shawl.

"If she told Ed Shaeffer she's not well," Alma remarked to her brother, just before going out the door, "put it down in your book that she's if anything rather bad."

Boyd frowned and shook his head.

A maid ushered Alma into the front room and then to a small elevator, whose existence had somehow slipped her mind, though when new it had been almost as much a subject of conversation in the town as Mrs. Barrington herself. The elevator took Alma directly to the spacious white bedroom where, seated on a four-poster, Mrs. B. herself looked alert and vigorous in a silk organdy dress, some color photographs spread out upon the counterpane before her.

"Your flag, my dear," the old monarch said, as Alma bent over to kiss her. "What on earth happened to that lovely old flag? It gave me such a start, I can tell you, not to see it out. I can't allow you and Boyd to run out on me, you know. You're all that's left!"

Alma laughed to see her old friend so full of herself.

134

"I'd have loaned you another, my stars," Mrs. B. said, on hearing Alma's explanation of the omission. "I've got a score in the attic. Why didn't you come to me?"

Alma's eyes strayed to the photographs on the bed.

"Put this thing away first, my dear," Mrs. B. said, handing Alma a magnifying glass with a light inside it.

"The photographs," Mrs. B. answered Alma's look of curiosity, "are the two lovebirds in Lisbon. Mr. and Mrs. Miller."

A somewhat sour laugh from Mrs. B. brought Alma up with a start.

"Sit down in this big cushiony affair," the older woman pointed to the chair nearest her. "You're such a dear to come to see an old moribund thing like me."

"Don't speak that way," Alma begged, no appetite for humor in her expression.

"You don't think I'd say I was dying if I thought I was, you fool," Mrs. B. told her. "My one fear, dear girl, is that I'm immortal."

Alma laughed.

"Look at the photographs if you wish," the old monarch said languidly. "I must say, Faye looks the best I've ever seen her. Vernon doesn't look so good. Dark circles under his eyes and all. Well, marriage is hard on a man."

"Do you suppose they'll be happy?" Alma said, turning one photograph quickly up after the other.

Mrs. Barrington stared at her.

"As happy as they would have been anyhow," the older woman finally replied, a kind of grimness on her mouth. Then going on, she said: "You know everybody has always claimed I have said such terrible things about marriage and the married. But that isn't quite true. I've said, of course, in my time, terrible things about nearly everything and everybody, but marriage is, I rather think, the one thing I always said I half-believed in."

To Alma's considerable astonishment, Mrs. B. opened a tiny gold box—it could only be a snuff-box—and too unconsciously for any attempt at display, dipped herself some snuff, then passed the box under the counterpane.

"My granddaughter, for example," the old woman continued, "thinks I am both inhuman and a hater of the married state only because when she complained about her husband's not being well-to-do enough to give her the ordinary comforts—she married a professor—I said to her, 'Accept the meanness and lack of satisfaction of being married. Why fight against something that is meant to try and deprive and deny and at last extinguish.' She didn't understand, of course, what I meant. Nobody knows any more that the thing that rewards the most is the most pain.

"But as to your question, Alma," Mrs. B. went on, "will Vernon and Faye be happy, I rather think they might. Vernon had no future with that poor devil Willard Baker, and Faye had no future as a college instructor and her mother's nursemaid. They both at least escaped from something fairly intolerable into marriage, which is often all marriage is for. And of course they're rich now. That always helps. They can go to North Africa and the Mediterranean or to the edge of hell and back when they're bored with each other and Rainbow Center."

Pausing briefly, Mrs. B. brought down her judgment with the decisiveness of the guillotine: "I guess poor Willard died at the right time as far as most of us are concerned." She caught her breath, then, as though she had regretted having, for the first time in her life, said the thing she had said.

Alma felt that Mrs. B. regretted her remark as indicating she felt callous about death in general and perhaps callous about Cliff's death in particular, but in the awkward silence that followed Alma could assure herself that this was not so. At the time of Cliff's death, Mrs. B. had written what is usually called a "beautiful" letter, from Washington. It *was*, in fact, a beautiful letter. It had been sincere, Alma was sure, but it came from such a distant emotional perspective, caused perhaps by Mrs. B.'s extreme age, that as an expression of sympathy it was too expert. Yet certain phrases in the letter showed unmistakably that Mrs. B. understood Alma's special grief and dilemma. Mrs. B. understood Alma, that is, and this disturbed the latter as much as it comforted her.

"Well, we needn't spend all of our Memorial Day talking about newlyweds," Mrs. B. said, handing the last of the photos to Alma. "Keep these if you like, or just put them on top of the bureau there when you're done with them."

Mrs. B. waited a moment and then said, "It's you I'm concerned about, Alma dear, and not Mr. and Mrs. Miller."

"Oh, I've begun to heal," Alma replied, startled a bit by the noticeable edge of bitterness in her own voice.

Taken aback a bit by Alma's having entered so abruptly into a subject which Mrs. B. had planned to prepare step by step in gradual and easy descent, the old monarch could only babble: "We haven't talked—not really talked—you know, my dear, for almost a year. I shouldn't have let anything keep me from you that long. Certainly letters don't count."

"Yours did," Alma managed to say.

"If your grief hasn't quite all healed," Mrs. B. began, a bit unwillingly, "then I hope your doubt has, or will."

"What about your grief and doubt?" Alma said, attempting to restrain her bitter edge, and perhaps unaware of any other than a rhetorical meaning to her statement.

Mrs. Barrington's heavy-veined hands pressed the counterpane a moment, but she did not hesitate to reply: "You have the right to ask that, if anybody does, though I hadn't planned for you to. I take it you refer to my marriage," she said, and then looking up sharply, "and *my* memorial."

"You were happy I'm sure," Alma said, her voice neutral. "You were loved."

"What makes you say so in that kind of voice?" Mrs. Barrington said, a deep and terrible calm in her tone.

"I only said you were loved. That's certainly true," Alma said.

Mrs. Barrington waited. "I didn't call you over here on a holiday exactly to talk about my marriage and my husband," she said, a kind of gray humbleness and melancholy in her manner.

"I've never known marriage or love," Alma said, and her voice was beyond bitterness.

"I couldn't agree with you less—about love," Mrs. B. said. The terrible look on her face had come back, so that Alma turned away. "I know you loved Cliff. I know his loss meant everything to you. But that's not the sorrow I see on your face, Alma. I know doubt when I see it, and I understand doubt. You don't know that about me, how could you, but I *know* doubt."

"Perhaps you do," Alma told her, and she sat back now like one who has taken a narcotic, her hands unfolding gently in her lap, like cut flowers which will only die.

"My nephew never loved me," Alma said at last.

Mrs. Barrington shook her head. Because darkness was gathering in the room, she turned on the lamp at her bedside.

"You loved him, though, my dear," Mrs. B. remarked.

Alma nodded.

"And you still do," the old woman said. Then waiting a bit more, she added: "That's all we dare hope for in this life."

"I understand that," Alma said.

"In your case, though, you can hope for more," Mrs. B. told her, in almost accusing tones.

Falling back into the pillows behind her back, the old monarch asked, "How could you presume to know he didn't care for you?"

Alma looked up like one who is about to hear a decision reversed by the judge of a higher court.

"Who told you he didn't?" Mrs. B. studied her face.

"I think it was Vernon Miller," the aunt replied at last, reluctantly.

"However would he know?" Mrs. B. remarked in a voice between ridicule and despair.

"There was a question of some money, you see," Alma began.

Mrs. B. nodded, waiting.

"Four thousand dollars," Alma told her.

Mrs. B.'s hands stirred under the counterpane.

"You know the story?" Alma inquired.

"Not all of it," Mrs. B. said, gaining control of her surprise. "That is, not all of it perhaps until now. I gave the four thousand dollars to Vernon—hoping he would, well, leave Willard Baker. . . ."

"Vernon gave it to Cliff," Alma explained.

Mrs. B. nodded, then said, "So Cliff could be free and run off for him, I suppose."

Alma lifted her hand to her coral beads, touched them inquisitively, and let her hand fall again to her lap.

"There's no doubt Cliff wanted to run off, Mrs. B. He wasn't happy in Rainbow."

"Run away from you, you mean," Mrs. B. inquired, testing the aunt's own frankness.

Alma nodded, lifted her hands, and let them fall to her sides.

"It's all over in any case," Alma said.

"Except that Vernon Miller didn't know the truth." Mrs. B. raised her voice slightly, not wanting her friend's deafness to assert itself here.

"You mean Vernon—" Alma began.

"Oh, no, he didn't lie," Mrs. B. interrupted her. "I don't think Vernon does lie. He's not very bright. He told you the truth as he heard it, but it wasn't the truth as your nephew felt it. Your nephew loved you, and he loved Boyd. He had nobody else to love, for one thing, though that's not the reason why. And his running away with Vernon's and my money, or without it, his wanting to run away, and all— who doesn't want to run away from those they love, and at his age? If I know anything," Mrs. B. looked at Alma out of her deep-set ancient eyes, "he loved you, Alma."

When there was no further response, Mrs. B. said, "You needn't believe me, of course. But I think you do, or will."

Relaxing in the silence that followed, Mrs. B. cleared her throat and continued: "I'm rather proud of Vernon, though, for giving Cliff the money. It shows, I think, he understood my gift, though he wasn't up to having it for his own."

"Cliff never used the money," Alma said. "We have it at home."

The old monarch nodded, waiting.

"You've had a loss which you don't yet understand," Mrs. B. said, suddenly taking out from under the covers of her bed a small fat thick book in Morocco leather. She half-opened the cover of the book, then closed it abruptly. "And I had a loss which in time I came to understand." She pushed the book out now toward Alma. "You see, I never wrote my memorial either."

Alma could only watch her, her hands on her beads.

"Please take it," Mrs. B. proffered the book of Morocco leather impatiently in Alma's direction.

The aunt rose ceremoniously and took the book from the old woman.

"I always wanted to tell somebody about *my* memorial, and I've never told anybody," Mrs. B. said. "Now it's too late. Once, you see, in the days when I still thought I was a writer, I planned to write about my marriage. The book I have given you is only a kind of record of what I planned. It isn't the memorial itself. Like you, I never wrote it."

"You never wrote it," Alma repeated, babbling.

Mrs. B. shook her head. "You see," she said, "my husband never loved me."

Alma began to say something, but the old monarch, with a look commanding silence, continued:

"When I heard you were writing the memorial to Cliff, I think I suffered everything over again in your place—why try to explain the mysteriousness of such a thing or its cause. I knew you suffered, in some obscure, different, and yet similar way to what I did. I knew what you suffered, Alma, and I knew what you lost . . ."

Alma wept now, silently, not for the nephew and herself this time, but for someone else. Mrs. B. allowed her to weep for a moment, her own face refreshed and reassured by what she had told.

"All the rest of my life," the old woman finished, "has been my trees and garden, and of course people. I have tried to give out love, piece by piece, Alma, charity, you know, blessed charity. Keep that book," she urged now pointing to the volume in Alma's hands, "if you ever think of me . . ."

Mrs. B. waited until silence settled again in the room.

"Here I've forgotten to serve refreshments of any kind!" the old monarch pointed out. "And we must both be dying of thirst and hunger."

She motioned for Alma to ring the maid's bell.

Alma shook her head. "I must be getting back to Boyd," she told her friend, and she bent down and kissed her.

"I had almost forgotten about Boyd for a moment," Mrs.

B. said. "I had thought that suddenly you and I, we two, were all alone in the world. I'm glad you've got him waiting though." Her last statement was perhaps too low for the aunt's deafness.

In a back room a tiny chime struck the hour.

"Before you go downstairs," Mrs. B. said, looking at Alma carefully, "I want you to go to my window over here on my left, and you look out at your house. Go ahead," she commanded. "I want you to look at how your wistaria falls over the side of your house. Do you see? There isn't a more beautiful sight in the country, Alma. Do you see what I see there? I spend a good deal of time now looking at it. Of course, I've always been partial to wistaria."

She looked away now from Alma to hide the look in her eyes, and picked up her snuff-box, and dipped.

"What did the old girl want?" Boyd glanced up at Alma from the pages of the holiday issue of the *Sentinel*. "You were gone one whale of a time!" He looked at his gold watch.

Alma held the Morocco leather book before her.

"Well?" Boyd said, irritated by her failure to answer.

"Oh, she was worried about the flag was all," Alma replied.

"I declare," Boyd laughed. "She's a card."

Alma sat down before the checkers table, from which the board had been removed, and laid Mrs. B.'s book down for a moment.

"Mrs. B. said she has a dozen flags in her attic and we could have just asked for one as easy as not."

"She's a great one for display," Boyd mused.

Alma saw that he was sleepy and his head hung heavily to one side, and it was already dark out, she had stayed that long at the old monarch's.

Then recovering himself suddenly with a start from his dozing, Boyd said: "Had a couple of visitors while you were out."

Alma nodded, glad he had not gone to sleep.

"They each of them brought you something," he told her. "One of them is a holiday surprise."

"Who came, Boyd?" Alma inquired.

"Emma Hotchkiss brought you her holiday special pineapple sherbert," he beamed, and Alma laughed. "And Professor Mannheim dropped in too. Brought you some old papers, I forgot what they are, he told me, but I don't recollect. He apologized for putting off bringing them so long."

Alma's eyes fell on a sheaf of yellow wrinkled notebook

140

paper on the easy chair near Boyd. She was glad Boyd did not remember.

"Can I get you a dish of the sherbet?" Boyd wondered. "Must be getting soft by now."

"Oh, I'd love a dish of that," she cried.

"You stay seated now, young woman," he seemed almost as limber as he got up. "I'll wait on you this time, hear?"

She smiled.

When he had gone out of the room, she rose suddenly, a sigh of pain and long suspense coming from her. Walking over to the chair where the yellow pages lay, she took them in the manner of one who picks up a hot iron. Hardly looking at them, she placed them with Mrs. Barrington's leather record book.

Going into the library, she quickly opened the drawer where she kept her own "memorial," and there she placed Mrs. B.'s leather notebook and the faded papers that had been Cliff Mason's schoolwork, covering both of them with tissue paper. Not trusting herself to look at them again, she closed the drawer, locked it, and put the key in her pocket.

"Where the deuce are you now?" she heard Boyd's voice.

"Oh, the sherbet already!" she cried, coming into the living room, and taking the dish from him.

"Better hurry up and eat it," he admonished her. "These home-made treats melt so fast, you know."

Sitting down in Mother's chair, she began spooning up the ice.

"Good, ain't it?" Boyd wondered.

"Just heavenly," she agreed.

They praised the sherbet, they mentioned the newlyweds in Lisbon, they smiled about Clara Himbaugh in Boston, and thought of Mrs. Hawke and Mrs. Van Tassel in South Carolina.

Alma insisted on washing the dishes and spoons and putting them neatly away.

Night's silence had settled in the room when she returned to her chair, and Boyd was already seriously dozing.

When his snoring woke him suddenly with a start, she heard her own voice say, "I'm so glad you've been here, Boyd. It would be pretty all-alone by myself."

There was a kind of odd fear in her voice that made him look at her before he said, "I can say the same, Alma," his voice thin and trebly in the dark.

"I've thought of Cliff a bit today, Boyd," she said at last, and she felt he nodded. "This was his day."

"You mustn't ever feel he didn't know," she heard his voice coming to her as if out of some eternal darkness. It was Boyd's old confident strong voice before he had got

141

sick. "Cliff knew we cared, Alma," he told her. "And that made him care too, at last, though he maybe never said it, and he didn't have the gift, you and I know, to write it."

There was no answer.

"Did you hear what I said?" Boyd asked. "Sometimes I think your hearing is nearly as bad as mine." He could only see her nod, not hear her voice.

By their practice of sitting in the dark, only their white hair which at times shone almost like phosphorescence betokened each other's presence.

Through the open windows there came the faint delicious perfume of azaleas. The court house clock struck ten.